Wir of the White Horde

Cheryl Burman

Guardians of the Forest Sequel

This is a work of fiction. Names, characters, businesses, places, events, locales, and incidents are either the products of the author's imagination or used in a fictitious manner. Any resemblance to actual persons, living or dead, or actual events is purely coincidental.

First published in the UK in 2023 by Holborn House Ltd.
©2023 Cheryl Burman

Apart from any use permitted under UK copyright law, this publication may only be reproduced, stored, or transmitted, in any form, or by any means, with the prior permission in writing of the publishers or, in the case of reprographic production, in accordance with the terms and licences issued by the Copyright Licensing Agency.

By Cheryl Burman

GUARDIANS OF THE FOREST
Trilogy
The Wild Army
Quests
Gryphon Magic
Prequel
Legend of the Winged Lion
Sequel
Winter of the White Horde

NOVELS
Keepers
Sequel
Walking in the Rain
River Witch

SHORT STORIES
Dragon Gift

www.cherylburman.com

Glossary

While *Winter of the White Horde* can be read as a standalone, a glossary is provided at the end of the book to serve as a reminder to readers of the prequel and trilogy, and to help new readers become familiar with the main races and characters.

Chapter One

Rebirth

This night was a new beginning, a rebirth. For twenty years she had nurtured the ashes of her magic, burned by that self-righteous king and his brat of a son.

Melda ground her teeth, reliving the humiliation. Skulking from the harbour at Etting – home to another enemy, one who betrayed his own father – having to ally herself with her enemy's enemy. She gazed, narrow-eyed, at the scruffy, greying ginger-haired man sitting on a rock by the fire, his slits of eyes narrowed further against the orange glare of the flames. The uncouth, loud Madach, Captain Jarrow, had served her well over the years. He arranged their passage west across the oceans, and on land he acted as bodyguard, hunter and provider of rough shelter on their journey to the High Alps of Asfarlon.

Melda allowed herself a thin smile. Asfarlon. She was right to seek the deep caverns, known to her through ancient books studied in her former life as a respected Seer of the Sleih people. Here, she was certain, lay the means to restore her powers. Magic hung in the air. Tiny invisible particles faded over centuries, yet alive enough, and eager to respond to her summons. They were paltry summons in the first instances, nurtured by the magic which in turn fed on her remembered spells – and on her deep, desperate quest for revenge.

With the magic came dulled spirits of Old Sleih, rising from the scattered rocks of their long imprisonment. Confused, their memories bleached by time, Melda bent them to her will. The first had been one who named himself Olban, a Seer from the time the Sleih inhabited the High Alps. The last had been a giant of a Sleih. He had no magic in him, only a strength Melda could harness. She frowned. Thrak, as the others called him, had been the most resistant to Melda's renewed ability to control the minds of lesser beings. He had succumbed in the end.

As they all would.

Triumph heated her heart. Soon, soon, they would all be in thrall to her. Once the gryphon pendant was hers, the ultimate source of power, they would be forced to adore her from prone positions on floors and earth. Serving her.

Rebirth. Melda strode to the fire, where the flames had died to expose lustrous, blazing gold and red coals. A quick glance at Jarrow and he rose from his rock. If he was to continue to serve her, she must instil some power in him. She pinched her lips. It would be little enough, given his dullard mind and suspicion of powers he could not see or touch.

Jarrow's eyes were glazed, his footsteps leaden. He moved like one wading through a teeming swamp, arms flailing as if to ward away the magic which swarmed and buzzed like angry wasps in the hot air. Futile. The magic would do to him what it would do. It must.

Melda drew herself up, tall and straight. She lifted the heavy bronze rod, forged by the spirits she had set free, in the fires she had rekindled. At the tip of the rod, a diamond glowed. She touched the diamond to the coals.

A vision of misshapen creatures, monsters of another time, racing across the alps filled her wide-eyed vision. Racing to her. Her white beauties.

'Great Spirit,' Melda cried. 'I set you free! Join with me!'

The flames roared high, brushing the cavern roof to scorch it black.

Chapter Two

Wishing for magic

On a late autumn day, Beron slouched at his desk in the school room. He concentrated on not listening to the new tutor drone on about the Danae, their history and culture, and their relationship with the Madach. Beron hadn't bothered to learn much about this race of small, stocky people living in a great dark Forest at the edge of a far northern sea. He didn't see why he should care about them. He was vaguely aware his father had once been friends with a Danae who became a Seer of the people called the Sleih. Beron hadn't been told how a Danae could have become a Seer because Father never said much about his life in the long ago time when he was young. Anyway, the Sleih in their beautiful Citadel far, far away to the north and the west, interested Beron far more. Seers interested him the most with their magic and power. It would be brilliant to have magical powers. He daydreamed about being a Seer. If a Danae could be one, why couldn't a Madach? Yes, he had a calling to be a Seer.

Or at least, something called him. Beron shifted in his seat.

The tutor sighed heavily. 'My dear boy, have you listened to a thing since the lesson started?'

Beron ran his fingers through his straight chestnut hair and smiled his charming blue-eyed smile which adults could never resist. He'd inherited the hair and the eyes from his mother, the daughter of a neighbouring Duchy, and tried hard to copy her easy charm. This tutor – the last in a long line – was proving more resistant than other adults. Beron liked him for not giving in too easily.

'No, sorry, sir.' Beron waved at the window where a golden late afternoon whispered, *Come and play. Join me.* The unknown woman's voice sounded real in his ear. 'It's the weather,' he said. 'I hate being stuck inside when it's sunny out.' He offered the tutor his most pleading face.

The tutor shrugged, smiling. 'I agree. Let's take a walk, shall we?'

Beron jumped up from the desk before the tutor could change his mind, which he was more than likely to do. Lessons never finished early.

'We can pay a visit to Dash,' the tutor said. 'See how he's getting on.'

Beron blinked. The tutor wasn't fond of horses. He didn't question the choice, however, thrilled with the idea. He loved Dash, even if the horse couldn't fly, like the horses of the Sleih. When Beron had asked his father for a flying horse, he had been told only the Sleih, or those with Sleih blood in them, could fly the big black horses. Beron had sulked at the unfairness. Those boring Danae, with their itsy bit of Sleih blood, could fly the horses and he, son of Lord Tristan and heir to the Duchy of Etting, couldn't. He had to settle for a black pony, plait its mane, paint its hooves, and pretend. He adored the little horse anyway, despite its shortcomings in the flying area.

Beron and the tutor pulled on boots and warm coats and ventured out to the stables.

That's right. Time to play.

The friendly voice encouraged him to hurry along.

'Dash needs exercise.' Beron might burst with the urge to mount the pony welling inside him. 'I have to take him for a ride.' He resisted crossing his arms and demanding to have his way. He'd learned arm-crossing and demands were unsuccessful with this tutor, which was a pity. Beron hadn't yet discovered what was successful.

'Hmm.' The tutor pulled at his chin. 'It'll be dark soon, and you're expected for tea with Lord Tristan and Lady Isabel.' He said this in an offhand way, suggesting it wasn't important.

Beron knew differently, but he had to mount Dash. The need to ride overwhelmed sensible thought, such as the consequences of being late for tea with his parents.

'A teensy ride?' he begged. 'A round or two of the stable yard?'

The tutor tossed a questioning look at the head groom, who said, vaguely, that if Sir Beron wanted a short trot around the yard, it wouldn't hurt. Why not?

Beron stared. The man wasn't usually accommodating. This afternoon, however, his normal stern expression had softened. Something wasn't right about his eyes.

The tutor lost interest in Beron's tea duties. 'Of course,' he said. 'Why not indeed?'

The stable boy, scowling at this addition to his work day, saddled the pony. Dash fidgeted and snorted. He expected oats, not exercise. When Beron led the pony into the yard, Dash snickered softly, nudging Beron's arm.

'Good pony, good boy, Dash,' Beron murmured into the horse's twitching ear.

The tutor and the head groom had their backs to Beron, a rare occurrence. They were deep in discussion about some matter.

Beron didn't wait around to be noticed. He stood on the mounting block and lifted himself into the saddle. His body buzzed with excitement, much more than a turn around the stable yard warranted. What he wanted, with all his heart, was to ride to the edge of the world. The voice murmuring in his head grew louder, more urgent.

Come, it called. *Come, join me.*

How could Beron join anyone if the grownups restricted him to the yard? He searched about. Ha! They had left the gate open. The two men continued to ignore him, their heads close together. The stable boy had disappeared.

Beron took the chance. He wheeled Dash about, yelled, 'Fly!', cantered off across the yard, and at the last minute spurred the pony to a gallop, out of the gate and into the lane which led to, and through, the estate's boundary walls.

Aghast shouts followed his escape. Beron giggled, patted Dash's plaited mane and kept galloping. He might gallop all the way to the edge of the world after all.

As he neared the wall, the voice called.

Beron, Beron, clever boy, come Beron. Join me.

Who was calling him? Over and over.

Hurry up, quickly, don't dawdle.

Why did the voice, so friendly before, now cause an uneasiness to settle deep in Beron's gut? The chill of near darkness fell heavily over him. He shivered. The edge of the world became less attractive. He pulled on the reins, wanting to turn back.

Dash ignored the tugs. The pony charged forward, along the narrow lane littered with autumn leaves, and through the gate which should have been bolted shut for the night. The open gate didn't help Beron's uneasiness. He yanked at the reins, calling for Dash to stop. They shouldn't be out here, in the dusk and cold.

At last, not far beyond the walls, Dash stopped abruptly. Beron clutched the pommel to stop from soaring over the pony's head.

Hello, Beron.

Beron wobbled in the saddle, pulled himself up straight, and stared. He'd found the voice, and he wasn't sure he was happy about it.

Ahead of him, on a low mound, a lady faced him. She wore a long blue cloak edged with silver, and was mounted on a fine, big black horse. Blue and silver ribbons curled through the horse's plaited mane, and its delicate painted hooves danced on the ground as if about to take flight. The lady's white hair was piled in braids on top of her head. Tucked into the braids, blue sapphires and diamonds set in silver glinted in the near dark.

She smiled at Beron, a warm, friendly smile.

Beron kept staring. She didn't appear to be a Madach.

Clever boy. I am not a Madach. I am Sleih, a Seer of the Sleih, such as you were thinking about a short time ago.

Yes, Beron had been thinking about his calling to be a Seer. How did the lady know? He was vaguely aware she hadn't spoken out loud. She talked to his mind – the same voice he had heard in the classroom and the stable yard. The uncomfortable feeling in the pit of Beron's stomach hardened, along with a whisper of scary excitement.

Come, we must hurry, before that dolt gets here.

'Hurry? Hurry where? Why?' Beron spoke out loud because he didn't like the lady knowing what he was thinking.

You do want to be a Seer don't you, with powers such as they have? Think what you could do with those powers!

Powers. Yes, Beron did want powers, to do something ... something great.

The lady's big black horse sidled alongside Dash. Busy thinking of greatness, Beron wasn't sure how he found himself astride the black horse instead of Dash. The lady shook the reins, spurring the horse along the lane outside the walls.

'Hey!' Beron shouted.

Blood pulsed in his ears. Notions of greatness evaporated. The feeling in his stomach solidified into fright, with no excitement. He opened his mouth to call for help. Nothing came beyond a strangled yelp.

Now the lady spoke out loud.

'Fly!' she called.

Her horse lifted into the air. Beron held tight, gasping with sick surprise. Shouts sounded below him. The ground was a dizzying distance away. Dash galloped along the lane, neighing, tossing his head, wild-eyed.

Behind Dash, the head groom rode a bay mare hard. 'Beron, Beron!' he cried into the darkening evening.

Dash and the mare were soon lost to distance and the failing light. The lady and Beron flew on, westward. A rising moon lit their way. Beron's heart beat frantically in his chest. What did this lady want with him? He suspected nothing good. How stupid he'd been to ride right into her trap. If he'd ignored the voice, he'd be having tea with his parents right now, safe and warm, and fed. He would give anything to be sitting at the table listening to his mother and father drone on about the affairs of Etting. Would he ever see them again?

***

'Blue and silver? A flying horse?'

Tristan's voice shook. He stood behind his desk, hands clasped to its solid edge to stop their shaking. Melda had been here. The disgraced, traitorous Seer had come to Etting and kidnapped Beron. His innocent son. A sharp coldness filled Tristan's body, his stomach nauseated.

'Do you know her, my lord?' the tutor asked. His voice wavered too.

'Yes,' Tristan hissed. 'An old enemy, once a Seer of the Sleih, a woman of pure malice, with reason to hate me and to hurt me.'

His mind whirled with nightmares of what Melda might do to Beron. He tried not to blame the tutor. The lady had played mind tricks on him too. On him, and his father. King Ieldon and the prince must not have completely destroyed her power, twenty years ago on Etting's docks.

'Will you organise a search party, my lord?'

Tristan brought his mind back to the urgent and horrific present. He gathered himself for the fight ahead.

'Yes, immediately.' He strode from behind the sanctuary of the desk, across thick rugs which warmed the stone floor. 'She may not be far.' As he said it, he understood how false was the hope, although she might need to be near enough to taunt him with messages, threats or ... worse. He shuddered. He must tell Isabel. A conversation which worsened the roiling in his gut.

He pulled open the door, called over his shoulder to the tutor. 'Find the steward, tell him what's happened and to gather men to search.' He stepped into the wide hallway where candles in sconces lit spaces empty of his father's plunder, shipped home to its owners. 'I will meet him and you at the stables. After I have spoken with Lady Isabel.'

Chapter Three

The view from the oak

Connor climbed high in the oak at the top of the ridge separating the Danae villages from the slope of forest at the edge of the oceans stretching south. Hoping the others wouldn't bother to search for him, he monkeyed from one familiar branch to the next. He had sort of inherited the tree from his Uncle Mark, like he'd inherited his uncle's copper-coloured curls and freckles. Mark had been the first to spot the Madach invaders arriving, when he was the same age as Connor was now. They had anchored their two big ships along the wooded shores, hauled out their axes and saws and set about felling the Forest to steal the timber.

Connor wouldn't give up his tree despite all the other kids' bullying, and even though he could easily be seen. The oak's once-sheltering summer leaves littered the ground with fading red, brown, and yellow, softening into a soggy mass with the drenching rains of the last days. The late afternoon was clear and cold. Tomorrow, the soggy mass would glitter with frost. Winter had arrived in the villages.

Arms stretched high, Connor's fingers found the branch he sought. He hauled himself up and sat astride it, rubbing his back against the rough bark of the trunk, before he remembered he was wearing his favourite jerkin – a present from Uncle Mark. If he dirtied or ripped it … He hated upsetting his beautiful, gentle mother, and ripping this jerkin would upset her a great deal. His uncle might be a grown man, yet his mother fretted about him all the time he was off soldiering with the prince from the Citadel.

The Citadel of Ilatias. Connor conjured the beautiful town with its tall, sand-coloured walls and towers with their bright flags. He had visited twice, once with his mother and once with Aunt Gwen. He loved the steep, winding cobbled streets, the busy markets with their tantalising food smells and colourful stalls. And the people! The Sleih with their gauzy, floating clothes, and the Madach in their sombre workaday garb. Connor imagined living there. He would study with Aunt Callie, learn to be a Seer like she was. He huffed quietly. No, he could never learn to be a Seer because, while he had his aunt's deep green eyes, he didn't have her Gryphon magic. The lack didn't stop him dreaming.

'Hey, Connor, we can see you hiding up there.'

Connor's shoulders stiffened. He ignored the taunting tone.

'Dreaming about flying horses and Sleih princes?' A second gibing voice joined the first.

'Why doesn't your witchy aunt cast a spell on you and teach you to fly?'

Snorts of hilarity. Connor's stomach churned. He hated it when his tormentors called Aunt Callie names. He had tried to tell them how Callie, a baby gryphon, and the wild animals of the Forest had saved the Danae from being sold as slaves. Aunt Gwen told him the story when he was old enough to listen, and many other stories too. He begged her to tell him more, devouring every one of her and Uncle Mark's adventures in the Deep Forest of Arneithe when they journeyed west to rescue his mother from the Sleih prince's enchantment. The other children had sniggered, telling him his family had great imaginations and should be story tellers, travelling the world with their fanciful tales. He stopped talking about it.

In his woody sanctuary, Connor kept his mouth shut. Before too long, the boys and girls would grow tired of their teasing, especially when supper called. Connor's stomach growled, and he grew chilled on his branch. He wished he'd worn a coat over his jerkin. He wouldn't leave until he was alone though, else the others would follow him home with their stupid comments, which would worry his mother.

At last, the children tramped off, jeering about people who imagined they could talk to deer and eagles. 'Hello, nice deer. Would you like to come home with me for supper? I mean, be my supper.' Hoots of appreciation.

Connor counted to one hundred before feeling his way out of the tree in the near darkness. His fingers were numb with cold. He shivered in his shirt and jerkin. Stupid not to have worn his warm coat and a hat.

He jumped backwards the last few feet to the ground and twisted about to take the path home. He stopped, stared. A tremor tickled his body before his brain caught up with what he saw.

A tall, black horse blocked his way. The horse's mane was plaited, entwined with blue and silver ribbons. Its delicate painted hooves pawed lightly at the ground as if about to take flight.

Connor's eyes lifted from the horse to its rider, a lady with glistening white hair piled high on her head and wide, deep green eyes much like his own. She wore a blue cloak edged with silver. His heart stopped. Aunt Gwen's stories tumbled around his brain. It couldn't be …? Could it? Not Lady Melda, the wicked Seer who tried to steal Aunt Callie's gryphon necklace. No. Her magic had been taken from her by the king and the prince. Uncle Mark saw it happen, Aunt Gwen said. Mark never spoke of it, or of those times at all.

You are Connor, son of Lucy, correct?

The lady stared into Connor's eyes. His head spun. He shifted his feet to balance himself.

She asked again, *You are Connor, son of Lucy, correct?*

Somewhere in Connor's befuddled head, he realised the rider wasn't speaking out loud. She spoke to his mind. Her grand appearance, with blue sapphires and diamonds set in silver tucked into her hair, told Connor she must be a Lady of the Sleih, even if she wasn't the wicked Melda. She was, though. He understood it in his gut, which clenched at the notion.

In the depths of his dizzying thoughts, Connor wanted

badly to run, as fast and as far as he could. Or climb into the oak, hang on to a branch and never let go. His legs were lead. His mind thickened. He couldn't think straight. He hesitated. Too long.

Somehow, he found himself thrown like a long sack across the saddle of the black horse, with the lady pushing his head into the animal's velvety side.

A pleasure to have you join me. The silent voice held mockery.

Connor wriggled, hard, tried to shout. The lady pushed his head harder into the horse's flank, with a strength beyond her slim body.

She shook the reins with her free hand and set off at a gallop along the track.

She spoke out loud for the first time.

"Fly!" she called.

The horse lifted into the air. Connor's stomach lurched. The track grew narrower, disappeared under the last of the brown leaves hanging from their branches. He shivered hard in the cold air. His heart thundered with fear. The horse flew west, over the Forest, into the red setting sun.

'Help!' Connor cried into the empty darkness.

***

Lucy pulled her cloak tighter, running along the dark lanes, past cottages where gaps in the drawn curtains glowed warmly with yellow candlelight. Wood smoke scented the air, overlaying hints of roasting meats and bubbling stews. The familiar homeliness gave her no comfort.

She had beaten on the doors of every child in the village who poked fun at her son. Irate mothers and fathers had glared when Lucy demanded their children tell her where Connor might be. At last, one young boy confessed.

'The old oak, the one on the ridge. We left him there at suppertime.'

Lucy had run to the ridge. Connor might have fallen, be lying unconscious. There was no sign of him.

There was a sign, however. The glint of a stone had drawn

her to where a tiny blue sapphire mounted in a silver clip lay in the damp, rotting leaves. Her stomach had somersaulted and sent her racing along the rutted track which joined the two villages, guided by the rising moon.

An owl flew low, its wings skimming Lucy's hair. She startled. The owl hooted softly, flew alongside her briefly. Lucy stood, panting, watching the bird. It rose into the sky, faced west, returned to Lucy, circled her, flew up, and west, hooting as it went.

While she couldn't understand the wild creatures like Callie could, Lucy had no need for a translation. West. She opened her clenched palm and stared with wet eyes at the jewel resting there.

Blue and silver. West. She swallowed bile.

In the smaller of the villages, she followed twisting lanes up the valley side until she reached the highest point, and the largest of the cottages. The curtains were drawn. White smoke rose from both chimneys.

Lucy hesitated. She needed to calm herself if she was to gain the help she needed. She banged the horseshoe knocker. Footsteps approached. The door opened.

'I need your help, Elder James.'

The grey-haired Elder's bushy eyebrows rose. He folded his arms over his fat belly. 'Help? I was about to eat my supper. Can't it wait until morning?'

'Connor has been stolen. By her.'

James peered at Lucy. She held his gaze, her lips trembling in their effort not to cry.

'Come in, come in, keep the cold out.'

Lucy followed the Elder into a cluttered, over-cushioned sitting room. A grey cat curled on an upholstered chair eyed her contemptuously before stretching and returning to sleep.

'What do you mean, her? And why do you think your son's been stolen?' James stood with his back to a leaping fire, hands clasped behind him.

'Melda, that's who I mean. The Sleih Seer who tried to steal the Gryphon pendant, with her ambitions for power far beyond Lord Rafe's. The lady in league with Jarrow to sell us all into slavery.'

James humphed. 'Those old tales?'

A weary hopelessness settled on Lucy. She shouldn't have come, to have to listen to this all over again.

'It happened, James,' Lucy said softly. 'You were here, you saw it.'

'Those silly tales from the time you were visiting this Citadel place and returned with your head, well, not quite right?' James smirked.

'I was there at the end.' Lucy stiffened, recalling her horror at arriving at the larger village to find it deserted, her dread that the Madach invaders had long taken the Danae away. 'I saw Callie and this Seer battle for the pendant, and Callie win, her and the gryphon.' The memory of her sister's strength, of Asfal the gryphon – named Child then, and a mere baby – inspired Lucy's courage. 'I saw the trees regenerate. All magic, Gryphon magic.'

'Humph.' James brought his toasted hands around to his front. 'So Callie and this woman had a tussle over a pretty chain. Women do that. As for gryphons! Wild imaginings.' His eyes were black holes under those eyebrows. 'The villagers understand there was no magic, how it was my brave intervention with Captain Jarrow which saved them. My negotiations, mine!'

Lucy waved her hands. This was old, futile ground, and time was precious. 'I've not come here to argue history,' she said, struggling to keep bitterness at bay. 'I've come begging help to find my son.' She held her voice steady. 'He's been kidnapped, and, I believe, is being taken west into the Deep Forest.'

'Kidnapped?' The Elder's voice tightened. 'This is what comes of filling the boy's head with wild tales. More likely he's run off, and you and your husband must deal with it. I don't have men to spare on wild goose chases. Now…' He strode to the door, opened it and ushered Lucy into the night. 'I'm sure he's already at home, having stayed out beyond his bedtime, and is wanting his supper.' He faced the kitchen from which warm smells came. 'As do I. Goodnight, Lucy.'

***

Gwen piled wood into the cooling range, listening to Lucy and Peter argue about how to find their missing son. She needed to be busy, do something to keep from thinking where Connor might be, what might be happening to him. Lucy had stumbled through her door as Gwen was clearing up after supper. She held her sobbing older sister, making sense of her garbled story.

'We best go to your place,' she had said at the end, holding back her own tears, letting her fury at James' self-serving insolence fuel her need for action. 'Peter will worry where you both are.'

'Melda? Are you sure?' Peter's voice told Gwen he wanted to deny it.

Lucy held out her palm, on which lay the blue and silver clasp.

Peter blanched. 'Ah.' His gaze roved about the tidy kitchen, searching for answers. 'Didn't the king and the prince take her magic from her?'

'Not enough of it, it seems.' Gwen shut the door on the crackling blaze.

Peter gave a sharp nod. 'I have to search for him.' Still in his coat and boots, he grabbed a lantern, lit it, and strode to the door.

'If she has a Sleih horse,' Lucy cried, 'they'll be well beyond finding.'

'I can't stay here, do nothing, while my son is out there – somewhere.' Peter gestured at the door. 'The wild creatures will help. You say they saw what happened. If he's anywhere near, they'll find him.' He drew a deep, calming breath. 'And if they don't, at least we can be certain …'

Lucy sat heavily in a kitchen chair. Gwen went to her, rested her hand on her sister's shoulder. 'I'll take Beauty and go to the Citadel. King Ieldon and Callie will know what to do.'

Chapter Four

Whispers

The whispers travelled from the north, riding the first snowflakes of winter. They piled themselves against the window of Callie's study, high in a tower in the Citadel of Ilatias.

She shivered, drew her shawl closer over her shoulders. She had become engrossed reading a book rescued from Lady Melda's library. Once it became apparent the lady was not returning to Ilatias any time soon, King Ieldon had ordered her house closed, the furniture covered. Rats, however, had invaded the stone, circular library, and King Ieldon worried for the safety of many priceless old manuscripts. Several had been given to Callie, including this thick tome.

She hadn't opened it for some time. Today she reached for it, unsettled by an unexplained urgency, a sense of pending trouble, to renew her knowledge of the contents. The book bore the cumbersome title, *The Ancient History of the Old Sleih and How They Came by Their Magic through Ponderous Schemes and Long Collusions with the Fabled Gryphon of the High Alps of Asfarlon*. Its faded blue leather cover was rubbed smooth and shiny. Much of the silver lettering was missing. The contents fascinated her. Handling its fragile pages with her fingertips, Callie read how the Gryphon pendant she wore was forged by ancient Sleih in the High Alps of Asfarlon and infused with potent magic by Gryphon and Sleih Seers. The thrilling tale told how a dread Evil rose from the depths below the High Alps, spreading terror in the Madach lands as monstrous creatures flocked to the Evil's summons.

Snuggling into her shawl, glad of the bright fire and the warm glow of lamps on the walls and her desk, Callie fingered the tiny silver gryphon with its blue head and green emerald eyes. The silver body, its tufted tail curled, lay on its side in repose, one sapphire blue wing rising up behind, the other closed against its flank.

A wondrous jewel in those far-off days, the book told how it was wielded by a Madach girl called Gweyr to defeat the Evil and set the country free from terror. The pendant's magic had dissipated over the aeons, yet sufficient remained to be of value to its wearer.

Who had written the book wasn't clear. Callie would have loved to find out. The blue and silver cover, favourite colours of Melda, suggested the author might have been the lady's distant ancestor. Without her evil.

The fire had died down while Callie concentrated on the book. Shivering, she stood to stir it into life, tossing back a stray black curl falling over her forehead. That was when she saw the owl on the window sill, peering in and fluffing its wings. It blended nicely with the snowflakes because it was white all over. Callie walked to the window and opened the casement for the bird to enter.

'Hello, old friend,' she greeted the owl. 'What news do you bring?'

Callie listened. Her mood darkened.

Bears and wolves racing across the High Plains, frightening the inhabitants of the scattered villages. Racing hard and fast to the High Alps, spotted by eagles as they sped, fleet of foot, across glaciers – before disappearing into deep crevasses.

Callie glanced at the book. Her shivers now were nothing to do with the cold of the room.

***

'It's so good to see you!' Callie hugged Tristan, wincing at the tightness with which he hugged her in return.

The two had been friends since the day Tristan's true, honourable nature won out over his duty to obey his empire-builder father in helping destroy the Forest where the Danae lived. Callie escaped the imprisoning walls which had been built around the village to live with the wild creatures, where she encouraged their frequent raids on the tree fellers. Tristan spied on his fellow Madach, sneaking away to warn her where they would next wield their deadly saws and axes.

'You, too.'

Tristan didn't smile. His normally sparkling brown eyes were tired and puffy, telling Callie his nights were restless. The crumpled state of his cloak suggested he had slept in it. Beneath the cloak, his clothes were in the same state. His brown curly hair was mussed, and he had shaved badly, as if combing his hair and shaving took time he couldn't spare.

Callie frowned, holding onto her questions, asking her housekeeper to bring hot drinks and food. She ushered Tristan into her sitting room. A fire burnished the rows of leather-bound books, and afternoon sunlight streaming from a high window lit paintings and tapestries filling the spaces between bookcases.

'Tell me. What's happened to bring you, in this state –' Callie gestured at the cloak Tristan tossed over the arm of a chair '– to my door, with no warning. In winter too.'

Her guest slumped to a book-laden sofa, not bothering to push aside the clutter. 'It's Beron,' he said in an exhausted, strangled voice. 'Melda took him.'

Callie's heart froze. Images conjured by the owl's news flooded her brain. The ancient book, too, with its cautionary tales. Melda. With her doubtless craving for revenge. All connected, it must be.

Tristan put his head in his hands. Callie stood beside him, her arm across his shoulders.

'We have search parties, useless,' Tristan mumbled. 'I left them and have travelled hard to come to you.' He lifted his head. Callie wanted to cry at the pain in his eyes. 'You saved me once, dear friend. Help me save my son.'

Callie's jaw tightened. Battling a vengeful Lady Melda would bring certain danger, yet … She tightened her hold on Tristan's shoulder. 'The saving worked both ways, and cost you dearly,' she said. She walked towards the hall. 'Come on. No time for hot drinks. We must see the king.'

***

King Ieldon paced the white-and-pink marble floor warmed by richly patterned rugs. Callie and Tristan stood by the sand-coloured stone fireplace, waiting for the king to take in their news.

'Twenty years,' he murmured. 'I had hoped to have longer than twenty years.' He stopped pacing, pulled his short beard, black despite his years, for the Sleih – at least those who use their magic – age slowly. 'The owl,' he said to Callie, 'worries me deeply –'

'Sire?' A servant had quietly come into the room.

'Yes?'

'A visitor, Sire. The Lady Gwen of the Danae.'

Her sister? Callie sensed more trouble. Gwen often visited the Citadel, spending time with her and the Sleih healer, Lady Clara. She always sent notice of her visits, however. And rarely travelled in winter. 'Gwen?' she said. 'Why is she here? She hasn't sent a –'

'Callie, thank the Beings I found you.' Gwen pushed past the servant, ignored the king, and threw herself into her sister's arms. Callie staggered with the force of the embrace, much as she had winced at Tristan's greeting hug.

Gwen stepped back. Her eyes carried the same weary, hopeless grieving as Tristan's. 'I went to your house. They said you'd left in a great rush, and Tristan –' Gwen glanced at him and then to Callie '– was with you, tired and anxious.'

Callie's uneasiness grew into tangible knowledge. 'Connor,' she whispered. 'Melda has taken Connor.'

Gwen's stifled sob told Callie she was right. Gwen gave Tristan a keener stare. 'Your boy, too?' Tears filled her eyes.

King Ieldon came forward and embraced Gwen as he would a daughter. They were old friends, adventuring together to stop Tristan's father, Lord Rafe, from razing the Forest and enslaving the Danae.

Gwen reached out her hand and lightly touched Callie's gryphon pendant. 'Will its magic restore our boy to us, like it restored Lucy?' she murmured.

Before the pendant displayed its true nature when it passed to Callie with her innate Gryphon magic, Gwen briefly wore the necklace. She had been the one the old Danae had given it to as a good luck charm during her and Mark's journey to find the Sleih and Lucy. Callie decided long ago wearing the charm gave her sister the touch of magic evident in her healing skills. Plus the tutelage of Lady Clara.

They needed more than healing skills now. As it would take more than the weakened jewel to bring back Beron and Connor. Callie grasped her sister's hand and brought it to her lips.

'We'll find a way.'

'You and Lord Tristan must refresh yourselves, eat and drink,' the king said gently. 'You will stay here as my guests.' He beckoned to the servant, standing by the door with a slightly furrowed brow. 'This man –'

'What's happening?' Princess Emeryn hurried into the room, her normal grace lost in friendly eagerness. 'I saw Gwen from the top of the stairs.' She twisted about. 'And Lord Tristan too. Too many years since you visited us, Tristan. Elrane will be sorry to have missed you all. Mark too, no doubt.' She stopped speaking, stared from one silent, anxious face to the next, and finally to the king, her father-in-law. 'A wonderful reunion.' Her voice faltered. 'Where is the party?'

'No party,' King Ieldon said. 'Rather, deeply troubling news.'

Gwen lifted her head from where she had been staring at the rug at her feet. 'Melda has our children,' she said. 'Lucy's boy, Tristan's son.'

'Melda?'

The king and Prince Elrane never talked about those times. Callie understood. Breaking the magic of a once-trusted Sleih Seer would have been harrowing and painful. Not a memory they wished to cherish. The princess and her two children had been told only that Callie was a Danae with strong magic of her own. She had found Asfal as a baby gryphon when his mother lay dying, and came to the Citadel to learn from the Seers and become a Seer herself.

'Old history. Grievous and terrible.' The pain in the king's eyes deepened. 'A former Seer who hungers for revenge on us all. Our children are her most potent weapons.'

The princess grew pale beneath her golden skin. Her deep green eyes widened.

'Our children. My twins?'

'Yes,' he murmured. 'They are safe within these walls. We must take care of course ... What is it, Emeryn?'

The princess stared at him. She lifted a slim-fingered hand to her mouth. 'Rowan and Willow are outside the Citadel. The sun, the snow ... They've taken the horses flying ...' She wavered. The king clasped her arm to steady her while talking urgently to Callie.

'Summon Asfal. If they have not returned, he will find them.'

Callie shared his urgency. If Melda found Willow and Rowan, the children would have no idea who the lady was, and no reason to flee.

The day was falling into nightmares which Callie had thought, like the king, would not rise for many, many years, if ever. She stood straight, her stomach fluttering. Lifting her shoulders, she called with her mind.

Asfal, we are in need. If you hear me, listen.

The answer came immediately. *Tell me what I must do.*

Chapter Five

'Well met'

'We should be going home, don't you think?' Willow called across to her brother, with little conviction. In this clear, sunny weather, the daylight held long enough to allow them more flying time.

'What's the rush?' Rowan shouted from his black stallion, Kez. 'This'll be our last proper ride until spring. Let's keep going.'

Willow stroked her young black mare's silky coat. 'You're having fun, too, aren't you, Dreamer?'

Dreamer lifted her head. Not in agreement. Willow felt the tug as the horse shied, moving sideways in the air. Willow's knees tightened. She yelped. 'What …?

Another rider flew towards them, the stranger's horse's hooves churning in full gallop.

Dreamer pawed the air, tossed her head. Willow held tight. Dreamer was named for her easy, relaxed nature. The mare had never acted like this before. Rowan had problems too, soothing a prancing, more excitable Kez.

'Who's there?' Rowan cried to the rider.

Children, children, well met.

The greeting came to Willow's mind. A Sleih Seer. She frowned, struggling with Dreamer, trying to think who this unknown Seer with powers of the mind might be.

You will know me well, hereafter.

The hint of gentle humour in the unspoken voice eased Willow's fright. Dreamer calmed too, treading air, waiting for the stranger to approach. Rowan had quieted Kez. He rode close to Willow, protective as ever.

'I think it's all right,' Willow whispered.

Of course it's all right. The humour strengthened. *I am an old friend of your grandfather, the wise Ieldon. Please send him my greetings.*

A friend of grandfather's? Willow relaxed further.

I have been absent from Ilatias for many years, travelling the world, learning new magic. I have recently returned.

Ah, that explained it. Likely Willow and Rowan were babies when this lovely lady left on her journeying.

The Seer joined them, riding between them. A tinge of uneasiness returned to Willow. She would have expected Rowan to object to the separation. Far from objecting, he gazed at the lady with adoring eyes. She was beautiful, Willow conceded, with shiny white hair upswept into coiled braids pinned with blue and silver jewels. Her golden skin was smooth, her green eyes wide and sparkling, smiling. Those eyes drew Willow … Her fright returned. The Seer was bending her magic on Rowan, herself, and the horses.

Clever girl. Magic flows from her, as graceful as her namesake. How lovely!

To bend another to your will using magic was wrong, forbidden. Willow, with stronger magic than Rowan, would soon start her training as a Seer. Seer or not, all Sleih learned this first law of magic at their mothers' knees – how none should force their powers of the mind on another unless in deadly trouble.

We will be friends, you and I, wise little princess. You will understand my mind as I understand yours. It will be sweet, wonderful.

Willow's mind misted over. It would indeed be wonderful to have a friend as powerful as this Seer. She screwed up her eyes. No, she mustn't succumb. This was wrong, terribly wrong.

With an effort, she wrenched Dreamer's reins, wanting to escape the Seer's magic. A pain blasted her head.

Oh no you don't, little princess. I have plans – 'Aaaghh!'

The lady screeched aloud, her horse dived, and Willow's mind cleared. A shadow fell over her and Rowan. She looked up, a new terror churning her stomach, and cried out with relief.

'Asfal! Rowan, see, it's Asfal!'

The great gryphon's rich blue-feathered eagle head and wings, and strong, tawny lion body, hovered above them. His tufted tail waved behind him like the banner of an advancing army.

Go, go, Asfal called. *I will deal with the Seer.*

Willow kicked her heels into Dreamer's sides. The mare responded, pushing forward. Willow twisted about, trusting Rowan had obeyed the gryphon. She gasped.

The Seer rode flank to flank with Kez. Her arms stretched out to grab Rowan, who gazed at her as unresisting as a newborn babe. Willow screamed, yanked Dreamer about, and stopped.

Asfal dropped from the sky like a lightning strike. His outstretched eagle talons raked the shouting Seer across her shoulders. His huge, hooked beak tore at her upswept braids like a bear ripping apart a bees' nest for honey.

The lady let go of Rowan. Willow couldn't breathe, terrified her brother, in his senseless state, would fall. She readied Dreamer to dive, held steady when Rowan straightened, clutched at his pommel as Kez carried his rider to safety.

Get away, hurry!

Dreamer and Kez galloped to the Citadel in the darkening evening. Willow's heart thumped, her head filled with awful imaginings of what could have happened.

Shrieks followed them. The Seer's furious voice filled Willow's head:

I will have vengeance. I will sit on the Sleih throne. That mindless boy will be my lapdog!

Chapter Six

Bound

Connor yanked at the ropes which tied his cold, sore body and his aching arms to a thick wooden pole embedded in the stony floor of the cavern. He wriggled his toes to ease his throbbing feet where more ropes bound his ankles. Firelight flickered from beyond an arched opening, and the smell of roasting meat tickled his nostrils. His stomach growled, his throat was parched. He hadn't eaten or drunk since lunch on whatever day it was the lady took him. Time was hard to keep track of in the dark and cold. More than ever, he wished he'd worn his coat when he climbed the oak. Except he hadn't expected to be kidnapped by a wicked woman on a flying horse and imprisoned in a cave. Let alone that wicked woman.

It had to be Lady Melda. How had she returned, with her powerful magic regained? And what did she want with him? Nothing good. Connor's head drooped to his chest. He would die here, never again see the Forest or his ma and da. A sob rose up his dry throat, threatening to choke him.

'Here, eat this.'

Connor jerked up his head. His eyes grew wide. A frightened boy stood before him, about two years younger than Connor. He was dressed in a thick, albeit grubby, well-made woollen jacket, leather trousers, and riding boots with fancy tooling on the sides. The steaming, delicious-smelling contents of a wooden bowl sloshed in his shaking hands. A matted fur was draped over one of the boy's shoulders, a water bottle peeping out from its folds.

'I can't,' Connor croaked. He wrenched at the ropes tying his arms.

The boy placed the bowl and the fur on the ground and picked clumsily at the knots until Connor could wriggle his arms free. He stretched them to the side, lifted his shoulders.

'My feet?'

The boy chewed his lip. 'He'd kill me. I'm allowed to give you these, and the water, and I'm supposed to be quick about it.'

'What's taking so long, boy?' The harsh shout echoed off the cave walls. 'Don't make me have to haul you out of there.'

'Gotta go.' The boy dropped the fur and water bottle where Connor could reach them and set the bowl beside them.

Connor lifted the bottle and gulped the brackish water. He didn't care about the taste. He spluttered, lowered the bottle, and peered at the boy, who remained standing there, staring. 'Who are you?' he asked.

'Beron. My father's Lord Tristan of Etting, which is why I think she took me.' He glanced at the opening. 'It seems that man, Jarrow, hates my dad, and this Lady Melda does too, whoever she is—'

'Jarrow? Captain Jarrow?' Connor recognised the name from Aunt Gwen's stories. He wouldn't have expected the belligerent captain to be here, with the lady. What did they have in common? Besides hating the Danae and Lord Tristan. Connor's fear grew.

'Stop the chat, you couple of old women.' A tall, heavy man with too-long, untidy curly hair and a beard to match loomed in the shadowy archway. He clutched a square dark bottle in one great paw and swayed gently.

Captain Jarrow. Connor's mouth went dry. Here, in this cave with him. The wicked Madach man who nearly succeeded in selling the Danae into slavery and destroying the Forest. A figure from a nightmare, shouting in the darkness. Connor shrunk into himself. The nightmare might ignore him.

'Get over here, you son of a traitorous dog,' Jarrow barked at Beron. 'Work to be done.' He rested his squinty gaze on Connor, who returned the stare with more bravery than he felt. 'Which one do you belong to, hey?'

Connor's heart pattered. What did the awful Jarrow want him to say?

The captain wove his way across the stone floor. He peered blearily at Connor, who twisted his head from Jarrow's stinking breath.

'The little witch?' Jarrow said. 'The troublemaker, the one who could order the beasts around? Her and her damn gryphon.' He poked Connor's shoulder with a black-nailed finger. 'Well?'

'If you mean my parents, sir, I don't see why I should tell you.' Connor wished his voice didn't shake. 'Leave them alone.'

A slap across his cheek wrenched Connor's head about. He gasped at the stinging pain. Behind Jarrow, Beron winced.

'Let me ask again, boy. Parents. Hey? You have the look of a Danae, so if not the witch, who? Who, who, who?'

Melda had known his mother was Lucy, Connor remembered. He could avoid another slap without betraying his family to this madman.

'My father's Peter, the miller's son, and my mother's Lucy.'

Jarrow scratched his filthy beard. 'The one who went crazy, stolen by the Sleih?'

'She did not go crazy!' Indignation conquered fear. 'The prince put an enchantment on her, and Aunt Gwen broke it with the Gryphon pendant—'

'That's what she wants, the pendant.' Jarrow grinned, and it was more terrible than the shouting, with a mouth full of brown and broken teeth. 'She'll have it too, with her magic back. And then—' he prodded Connor's shoulder harder '—your lot will end up where you should have ended up the first time.' He crossed his arms across the food-stained shirt covering his beefy chest. 'Slaves in the holds of my ships.' With a grating chuckle, he stumbled through the arch.

'I know who Jarrow is, and your dad,' Connor whispered to Beron, who stared at Jarrow's back. 'Your dad was friends with my Aunt Callie, helped her save the Forest, and our people. I know it all. Didn't your dad tell you?'

'Not much. He doesn't talk about the past.' Beron bit his

lip. 'Is the lady really dangerous?'

'Oh yes.'

Another shout sent Beron scuttling off. Connor peered at the cooling stew, lifted it to his dry lips, took a mouthful, and another.

Aunt Callie wore the Gryphon pendant. If this Lady Melda was desperate to have it, if her magic had returned... it seemed she would stop at nothing to get her revenge.

Connor pushed the food aside, his hunger gone in the face of his horrifying imaginings.

***

I know who Jarrow is, who your dad is. I know it all.

All what? Beron hunched in a shallow crevice in the cold wall. While the warmth of the huge fire couldn't reach him there, neither could Captain Jarrow's shouting, fist-waving temper. He snuggled into his coat, discontent rising in him like bile.

How unfair life was. This Danae boy had been told everything about the time Beron's father became friends with the girl who was probably the one who was a Seer in the magical Citadel. All the stories, all the people, good and bad. Beron had been told nothing, and was in this awful danger because of his ignorance.

He wriggled on the hard floor, his self-pity tarnished by a speck of guilt. Recognising the lady hadn't saved the Danae boy, who was in a far worse position than Beron. Tied up, given barely any food or water. Jarrow hated him, talking about witches and slaves. Jarrow hated Beron's father too, always shouting about the traitor. Connor said Beron's dad had saved the Danae from slavery. A grudging respect slipped between the self-pity and the guilt. A hero for a father. Beron squared his shoulders. If the chance came, he'd try to be a hero too. He would. If he could, because he had to admit he was very scared.

By the fire, the captain put aside the square bottle and rolled himself in his filthy blankets. His snores soon echoed in the vast space. Beron crawled out from his shelter. He stared at the stone steps leading out of the cave, into the pitch blackness of nightmares. Should he try to escape? With no light, no idea where he was, or where the stairs led? He trembled at the thought of being lost in the caves. No. With no guide, the tunnels offered no escape. He crept into his hiding hole, and cried himself to sleep.

Chapter Seven

Eavesdropping

That mindless boy will be my lapdog.

Willow rolled onto her stomach and buried her head in the feather pillow. The Seer's vicious threat played over and over in her mind. Sleep was impossible.

Asfal had caught up with her and Rowan as they neared the Citadel, their horses exhausted, driven on by the same terror pounding Willow's ribs. Rowan had regained his senses enough to share her fright, urging a willing Kez forward.

The second they alighted in the courtyard by the stables, their mother ran to Willow, helping her off Dreamer and squeezing her tightly. Grandfather lifted Rowan to the ground and peered carefully into his eyes. He frowned, ran his hands over Rowan's dark head, and finally smiled softly. He murmured words which made Rowan's golden skin deepen with a blush.

Then he gazed at Willow, who opened her eyes and her thoughts to her grandfather.

'Ah.' Grandfather's eyebrows arched. 'She said that, did she? Old friends indeed. Once, it was true.'

Willow heard his sadness, and her curiosity about the Seer grew. She caught the whisper of a name – Melda – before Grandfather's memories closed to her.

He patted her shoulder. 'Well done, Granddaughter. You resisted her well, no mean feat. I'm proud of you both.'

Willow's cheeks had heated. Grandfather did not praise lightly.

Tossing in her bed, wide awake, Willow needed to find out more. She would go to Grandfather and ask. He'd tell her.

She pushed off the quilted cover, slipped her feet into soft wool boots, her arms into a thick robe, and crossed the room to her door. No need for a candle, the passageways would be well lit. Likely, Grandfather would be in his study, which proved to be the case.

Not alone, however. As Willow neared the open doorway, voices fell into the passage. Worried voices. One belonged to her mother.

Willow blew out a frustrated breath. No point going in, they would send her to bed. She took a step the way she had come. And stopped, ears pricked like a pony waiting for sugar.

'The message is clear, Emeryn. Melda wants the pendant for the children.'

Melda. The name Grandfather murmured in his thoughts.

Message? Children? Pendant? Willow glanced along the empty passageway. She crept to the doorway and pressed herself to the rough warmth of a tapestry hanging on the stone wall.

'She expected to have Rowan too.' At first puzzled, Willow recognised the voice as belonging to Gwen, Callie's sister and Danae healer. Winter was an odd time for her to visit.

'Yes,' Grandfather said. 'The message she planted in Rowan's mind would have been sent with Willow, a warning in itself that the girl would do her bidding.'

Willow's stomach grew queasy, recalling her misting mind, her desire to have the Seer as a friend. Thank the Beings for Asfal's rescue.

'We cannot, of course, give up the pendant.' Her mother was firm. 'We must wait for Elrane's return, which will be swift now he has been sent for.'

An unfamiliar voice joined in. 'Princess, with respect, that is easy for you to say. It's not your son being held in whatever prison this evil woman has made for him.'

The Seer held the man's son? Why?

'Or your nephew, as she does mine,' Gwen said, more gently than the male voice.

Nephew? Ah yes, the boy with red, curly hair and green

eyes, about Willow's age. She had met him twice and liked him very much. A Danae with a spark of Gryphon magic she had thought at the time, wondering if she was mistaken when no one else commented.

'Forgive me, of course.' Her mother, ashamed.

Willow's brain worked hard. This Melda had planned to have three boys as her prisoners, to bargain for a pendant. Did they mean the Gryphon pendant Callie wore? Willow knew the jewel and some of its aeons-old history. But the pendant's once powerful magic had waned. Why did the lady want it?

'Sadly, you are right, Emeryn.' Grandfather's grave voice spoke his sorrow. 'We cannot allow her to have it.'

'She has them in the caverns of the High Alps.' Callie was in the room, sounding certain about where the lady held the two boys. 'She won't harm them. We can be sure of that.'

'Not until she has what she wants.' The male voice was sharp with despair.

A knot formed in Willow's throat, thinking Rowan could have been there too. Those poor boys.

'Why the High Alps?' Gwen asked.

'Yes, why there?' the stranger added.

Grandfather answered. 'The Sleih and Gryphon once lived in caverns within the High Alps of Asfarlon. It's where the gryphon pendant was forged,' he said, 'and imbued with Gryphon and Sleih magic as a weapon to vanquish a demonic Evil which skulked in the depths below.'

'We know the history,' Callie said, 'because someone wrote it down in a book which has survived, and which Melda owned.' Callie's voice faded and grew louder, as if she was pacing the room.

'Callie has had news,' Grandfather said, 'of disturbances in the High Alps, which lead us to believe Melda is there.' He paused. No one asked what kind of disturbances. 'If she gains the Gryphon pendant,' Grandfather went on, 'if she has woken the Evil which has lain dormant for centuries … if she brings the two together …' He trailed off as if ending his sentence would bring about catastrophic horror.

There was silence for a heartbeat, two, before Callie said, loudly, 'Is it your wish, Sire, that Willow be a party to our discussions? For–'

Willow stepped back in fright as Callie loomed in the doorway, arms crossed.

'I'm sorry,' Willow blurted. 'I wanted to ask Grandfather what was going on and realised if I came in, Mother would send me to bed.'

'Which is where you should be.' Her mother tutted softly, took Willow by the arm and steered her along the passageway. 'Tonight you need rest. Tomorrow, I will ask your grandfather to tell you and I, and Rowan, all about this Melda person. I promise.' She let go of Willow's arm, slid it around her waist, and squeezed gently. 'Time to sleep, my precious daughter.'

Willow had no choice.

***

Those left in the king's study were well acquainted with this Melda person in the days when she was a respected Seer on the King's Council – before revealing her ugly ambitions.

The king stood before the fire. Gwen and Tristan sat on the edges of their chairs. Without reading their thoughts, Callie understood her sister and friend waited anxiously for instructions, for words of wisdom, and for comfort. From her seat under a window, she gazed absentmindedly at the snow heaping itself on the stone ledge. She thought of the owl and its news. Her heart ached for Connor and Beron, imprisoned in the cold depths below the caverns.

'Asfal will carry me to the High Alps,' Callie said. 'We can rescue the boys.'

'And become captive yourself?' Gwen threw up her hands. 'Carry the pendant straight to her?'

'The pendant will stay here.' A frisson of fear ran through Callie as she spoke the words. 'We can't risk it. Besides, Asfal has proven he can send her fleeing. Maybe–'

'Ieldon. I carry a message.' The voice cut sharply across Callie's words.

She gasped at the sight of the servant standing in the doorway. Shoulders hunched, he cringed like a beaten dog. His eyes shifted about the room, unfocused, frightened, in chilling contrast to his voice, which was strong, clear, with a tinge of mockery.

Melda. This was her calling card. Indignation and fear mingled in Callie's heart.

The king gently cradled the messenger's head. The man's eyes rolled into their sockets.

'Tell me,' the king said softly.

'The pendant for the brats. Else they die. You have my word as a Seer of the Sleih.' The servant delivered his message in the same mocking tone.

King Ieldon peered into the messenger's face for a long time. Callie waited, anxious, hoping. Finally, the man relaxed, slumping in the king's hold. Tristan caught him and supported him to a couch. Gwen hurried over, reaching for the messenger's wrist to feel for a pulse.

'Melda proves her renewed power once more, Sire,' Callie said.

'His body will recover.' The king's voice was cold, hard. 'His mind will not.'

Callie's stomach roiled, thinking what this might mean for the two captured boys, even if Melda did not kill them. Gwen's and Tristan's pale faces told her they too understood the sinister, deeper message.

The king pivoted on his heel. 'Lord Tristan, you must trust us to rescue your son. You yourself should return to your people, prepare them for a possible attack.'

Tristan hesitated, glanced at Callie, who gave a short nod. 'I agree, Sire,' he said, 'though it breaks me to leave here without Beron.' He rubbed a hand over his tired eyes. 'Something in my gut tells me Melda has plans for Etting. It was, after all, the scene of her humiliation.'

'You also, Gwen,' the king said. 'The Danae are in danger too.'

Gwen lifted her head from examining the unconscious man.

She frowned. 'How can I go home to Lucy without her son?'

'There's nothing you can do here,' Callie said, sick with feeling for her oldest sister's grief. 'You can do more good warning our people, save lives perhaps.'

Gwen reached out to clasp Callie's hand. Tears welled in both their eyes. 'You promise me you will leave nothing left undone to find him?'

'I promise.'

The king held himself stiffly, hands clenched at his sides. 'I was a fool to think she would cause no more trouble. I should have stripped her of more than her powers when I had the chance.' He brought his hands up to press his fingers into his temples. 'Although a terrible thing to do, I should have taken her mind, just as she did to poor Lord Rafe.' Lowering his hands, he took them all in. 'This is my doing, and I must make it good. Tristan, Callie, Gwen. If we are to bring those boys home, and save our people from Melda's malice, we must defeat her–' he paused '–utterly and completely, this time.'

Chapter Eight

Melda's Malice

'I will crush them under my feet. They will be my mindless pets!'

Connor curled into the matted fur Beron had left him, shrinking from the Seer's vicious threats screamed from beyond the arch. Other voices joined her in a ghostly, malicious chant which raised shivers on Connor's spine. These were the wraiths the lady had summoned from the darkness of the cave. Beron had whispered it to him one night as the two of them huddled against each other, watching shadows writhe on the rocky walls in the far cavern.

'Obedient to the core! Won't they be, my pretty little lord?'

In the silence which met Lady Melda's harsh tones, Connor imagined poor Beron nodding his agreement. When the lady was in the caverns, Beron trailed her like a dazed, witless puppy. At other times, he was as lucid as a terror-struck young boy could be, given a spiteful Jarrow delighted in feeding him lurid ideas of what Melda planned for her captives.

'The pendant will be mine! I will have it from the little witch.'

The chanting rose at the mention of the pendant, and Jarrow grunted his support, swearing at the witch's demon and its attack on the lady.

Witch's demon? If the witch was Aunt Callie, the demon must be the gryphon. Connor had never met Asfal, which didn't stop him dreaming what it must be like to share the mind of such a wonderful beast. He filled his thoughts with imagined pictures of talking with the gryphon, hauling at his courage to drown the frightening curses filling the air.

'You, son of the pretty, enchanted fool!'

Connor was shaken from his imaginings. The lady stood over him, glowering. He kept his head down. Safer not to meet her eyes. She grabbed and lifted his chin, and there it was – the dizziness. He forced his eyelids shut. They sprang wide. Clouds rippled in his head.

'Ha! You think your dull speck of magic can be used against a Seer of the Sleih?' Melda's voice was kind, softened with laughter. Connor wanted to laugh too. How silly of him to think he could do anything except the lady's bidding. And why would he not want to? If he obeyed her, she might untie him. Beron wasn't bound. Why did the lady insist Connor should be?

'Tell me, boy,' she said, making the word boy a caress, 'are there others among the Danae with the witch's strength of magic?'

Connor baulked. Aunt Callie wasn't a witch. He didn't want to answer. He shut his mouth tight. The lady grunted, and Connor's lips parted. 'No, nobody.' He choked on the words, which flowed anyway. When she squeezed his chin more tightly, he understood he needed to – wanted to – tell her everything.

'Only Aunt Callie, if you mean her, and she's in the Citadel.' Connor held his sore shoulders higher. 'She's a Seer, and one day she'll serve on the King's Council.'

'A Seer, in the Citadel. Well, well.' Her pale lips lifted in amusement. 'Perhaps dear Ieldon has shared my message with her, delight them both.'

The lady's voice was smooth as cream. Connor could listen to her forever.

'There are no others?' She probed his mind, gently searching. 'Yes,' she murmured, and Connor was happy to give her what she wanted. And more. 'Hmm,' she purred. 'The Danae have forgotten what happened? This … James, Elder James … it was he who saved them from Jarrow and his slave ships?'

She abruptly let go of Connor's chin. It jerked to his chest.

'They are undefended,' she called to Jarrow as she marched away. 'And it seems your old ally, James, has re-written history.

You will have your fairytale slaves.'

The whirling mists in Connor's mind cleared with a searing jolt. Fairytale slaves! What had he done, laying bare the Danae's lack of defence? He wanted to be sick.

Every child in the two villages was taught the story at their mother's knee, of how the Danae came to be considered a fairytale. Connor pressed into the cold stone, hearing his mother's gentle voice telling the story.

'Long ago,' she said, 'the Danae were banished from the Sleih kingdom. The told tale was the Madach wanted our lands.' She would give a hiccup of a laugh here. 'Do you remember what Aunt Gwen told us? The truth she learned from old Josh, the Danae she and Uncle Mark met in the Deep Forest?'

Connor's murmured 'Yes' never stopped her telling the rest of the story, for which he was grateful.

'Seems we are part Madach and part Sleih, but sadly'–his mother never sounded terribly sad at this bit–'the Danae have barely any magic and no great strength like our Madach cousins. We were, frankly, an embarrassment.' Her soft chuckle delighted him, before her voice grew serious. 'They sent us east into the Deep Forest of Arneithe to make new lives. We were forced to travel a harrowing journey among trees which never welcomed us. We lost many along the way. Yet we went on until the ocean stopped us going further.' She would stroke Connor's hair from his forehead. 'Hidden from the rest of the world, we faded into memory as a myth, a fairytale.' She would pause, humph. 'Which delighted the Madach Captain Jarrow when he discovered we actually existed.'

A tremor would run up Connor's spine, thinking of the fate the Danae narrowly avoided at the greedy captain's hands. 'He planned to sell us to Madach lords and ladies who'd rush to buy fairytale slaves at any price,' he would whisper. 'He'd grow rich.'

'But he didn't,' his mother would say, smiling. 'And now it's time for sleep.'

No sleep for Connor in this cold cave. The captain's rantings showed his ambition had not been dulled over twenty years.

Rather, it was strengthened by revenge against those who thwarted him. And Connor had told him his old ally Elder James was still there, and the Danae no longer remembered the magic which saved them. They trusted the Elder, as they did before Jarrow and his soldiers and tree fellers arrived on the Forest's shores.

Connor couldn't warn them, could do nothing. Escape was impossible tied to this pole in the cold and dark, with endless black tunnels the one way to freedom. He pulled the musty fur tight about him and cried softly into its folds.

***

Is this wise?

In answer, Callie clamped her legs to Asfal's tawny sides as tightly as she could. She rarely rode the gryphon. While Asfal might not have minded, Callie's respect for his kind stopped her from treating him as she would a horse. Besides, she had a horse.

'Our combined strength will keep us safe,' she reminded herself as much as the gryphon. The pendant which might, possibly, have given them true protection from Melda sat in a wooden box inside an iron chest in the Citadel's treasury. Callie felt its absence like a missing limb.

The Citadel, the snowy fields and woods surrounding it, and the High Plains with their scattered villages showing as dark splashes staining the blue-shadowed snow, were behind them. The foothills of the High Alps of Asfarlon unfolded, trees became rarer, and Asfal flew between rocky cliffs and above frozen glacier lakes, rising higher as they neared the peaks. Callie was glad of her heavy cloak, woven from the wool of mountain goats and imbued with magic to give it greater warmth – and enhance the wearer's own magic.

The air. Do you sense it?

Callie sniffed. The coldness of the air froze her nostrils. And something else. A scent, unpleasant, at the edges.

'Yes, a nasty smell …'

Evil. See? Below the rocky ledge.

Asfal tilted sideways, and Callie's grip tightened. A pack of white wolves with too-big heads and misshapen bodies skulked under the ledge. When Asfal flew lower, the wolves abandoned their shelter to leap at him, snapping and howling. Their chilling cries hurled a warning: Stay away.

Let's leave them alone, Callie silently urged.

Even as Asfal swung about, a white miasma rose, swift as birds' flight, from the wolves' red-rimmed mouths. Tendrils curled, reaching for Callie. She curled tighter against the gryphon's neck as Asfal twisted out of the miasma's path. He rose higher, crested a ridge, and they were above a wide, ragged-edged glacier. It flowed like a blue and white scar between snowy, rocky slopes. Callie eyed it with suspicion. She recognised this glacier.

The book she had borrowed from Melda's library told how, centuries ago, an army of deformed white bears, wolves, giant cat-like creatures and other horrors rose from this glacier's crevasses to lay siege to the caverns of Asfarlon where the Sleih and Gryphon lived. Mindless, vicious, they were the creatures of the Evil which dwelt in the depths of the mountains.

There. Asfal flew lower over the ice. *What abominations are these?*

Callie gasped as the nightmare of the old book lived before her eyes. Monstrous creatures raced across the icy ridges as smoothly as if the jagged glacier was a summer meadow. Hump-backed, crooked legs, some with one giant eye in the centre of their faces – what once might have been wild creatures. What once might have been people.

Callie's stomach revolted. Was this to be the fate of the boys? Her and Asfal's fate if they stayed?

The same white mist which the wolves had breathed rose from the yowling, snapping, leaping creatures. Once more, its writhing tongues sought Callie. Asfal flew higher. The mist followed. The highest of the swirling vapours touched Callie's cloak, where they hissed a death in the arms of the magic there. She pulled her hood closer over her head, pressed herself into Asfal's feathers. Disgust and fear mingled at the idea of a single drop reaching her skin.

Come, little witch. Welcome. Melda's sneering tones wove through the miasma. *See my new friends, how well I treat them. What I plan for them.*

The words tugged at Callie. Every emotion screamed at her to follow the voice, find the boys.

Hold, dear heart. Close your ears. Asfal's warning shook Callie into sense.

We're not enough to battle this by ourselves, she said. *Not this time. It will be death or ... worse.*

Hang on, the gryphon warned.

Melda's goading followed them through the poisonous mist as Asfal flew in a tightening circle, spiralling upwards, a hurricane of blue feathers and golden fur, and then –

Keep holding, tight as you can –

He spun out of the spiral, flung himself out and over the crest, above the guarding wolves, and raced for the Citadel.

Callie's nerves stayed taut until the towers of Ilatias were in view, their sand-coloured stone glowing a warm welcome in the winter afternoon's subdued light.

Asfal landed in the courtyard by the stables, and Callie slid off him. Her legs trembled. The images of what this Evil, using Melda, had created, appalled her. 'Did you hear?' she said.

Yes, dear heart. Asfal bent his eagle head around to nudge her with his golden beak. *I heard her.*

'Her cruel voice, chanting, *This is war.*' Callie shuddered. 'War against those monsters.'

***

Beron grew thinner, his eyes glassy. Each time the boy brought Connor food and drink, he said less, laying the food and water on the floor and scuttling off as if devils were on his tail. Connor's spirits sank, watching him. Neither of them would ever see daylight, let alone their families. If a miracle happened and they did escape, what state would Beron's mind – or his own – be in? At night he cried himself to sleep, if night it was.

Jarrow laid a heavy hand on Connor's head. Connor stiffened, waiting for the blow. It didn't come.

'She says I can untie you.' The captain grinned.

Connor's relief lasted until the malicious glint in Jarrow's beady eyes doused it.

'You'll be free.' Jarrow sniggered. 'Of sorts.' He shouted through the firelit arch. 'Boy, get over here.'

Beron hurried in, stood stiffly by Jarrow's side. 'Yes, sir.'

'Put this on him and then untie him.' He handed Beron a wide, brown leather collar attached to a chain.

A collar? Like a dog? The collar was high, designed to cover the whole neck of, say, a boy. A metal buckle secured it. Connor gulped. He would have fought having that suffocating piece of leather around his neck, except Beron would be in trouble, and it would happen anyway. He eyed the spacing of the holes where the buckle's prong would go. The collar would be fastened more tightly if Jarrow did it.

Beron fumbled with the stiff leather, finally, clumsily, slipping it around Connor's throat and buckling it. He left it loose, but once the buckle was in place, the high collar stiffened. Connor cried out. Tiny, sharp points on the inside jabbed at his skin like a hen picking at corn. What? No studs had been visible when Beron struggled to fit the collar in place.

Connor stared up at Jarrow. 'What does the collar do?' His voice quivered.

'Do?' Jarrow yanked on the chain and Connor yelped. 'It keeps you from wandering, if there was somewhere to wander to.'

'Is there poison on it?' Dread filled Connor's mouth and the words were hard to say.

'What you talking about?' Jarrow scowled. 'Be quiet and let the little lord untie you.'

Beron picked at the knots. They refused to come undone after days of being pulled tight by Connor's struggling. Jarrow grew impatient, growled, 'Out of the way,' and sliced apart the knots with a knife. Connor cried out. Spots of blood pooled on his ankles where the knife had grazed his rubbed-raw skin.

'Stand up.'

Connor's legs buckled when he tried to obey. Jarrow grunted. Connor tensed, waiting to be hauled bodily by the chain across the stony floor. His pulse pounded. He wouldn't let it happen, he couldn't. He squeezed his eyes shut, breathed in. A spark of courage lit inside him, a golden glow. He pushed himself up. He trembled.

'Hold on to me.' Beron was by his side, offering his shoulder, avoiding Jarrow's glare.

Connor leaned into the boy and the two of them wavered, steadied. Connor's legs held, and he eased his full weight off Beron.

Jarrow snorted. 'Little hero, hey?' He tossed Beron the chain. 'Here you go. You can walk your pet to his new home.'

Jarrow stamped across the floor, Beron and Connor following him into the cavern where the captain spent his time.

Connor gazed about the immense space as best he could with the restrictive collar. The roof disappeared into darkness despite the mighty fire which roared in the middle of the cave and the occasional flaming torch. Dark streams of slime glistened on the dank walls, giving sustenance to sponge-like black plants thriving thickly on rocky ledges. Below and between the ledges, the walls curved in and out to form alcoves of different sizes. A sickening odour of decay, like rotting meat, tinged the cold, damp air.

Rough wooden bars enclosed many of the alcoves. Connor gaped. A press of hideous white creatures paced behind the bars. Those with hands grasped the wood with fleshless fingers. Others pushed their heads against them, teeth bared, snarling. Connor shuddered as waves of the scent of unwashed skin and decaying hides flowed from the alcove prisons.

What were these creatures? Where had they come from?

A hollow snigger drew Connor's attention to ghost-like people – the wraiths Beron had told him about – who hovered near the fire as if its warmth could restore blood to their veins. Goosebumps rose on his arms.

The tallest of them stared at him. 'A student?' The gravelly whisper made Connor grit his teeth. 'Such poor material to work with.'

'Seer Olban,' Jarrow said, and he sounded respectful, 'the boy is a prisoner like this one.' He cuffed Beron's head. Beron blinked. 'Why my lady insists on chains and cages, I've no idea. He could be useful, like the little one.' He cuffed Beron's head again.

'You don't see it, do you?' The wraith, Olban, appeared in front of Connor, squinting into his eyes. 'A spark. The best she has to work with, unfortunate lady.'

Olban returned to the group by the fire, leaving a stench of oily ash which clung to Connor's skin, setting it tingling with disgust. He wanted to ask what the wraith meant about sparks and students. He couldn't. Jarrow grabbed the chain from Beron and pulled him towards the caged beasts.

'No!' Dread beat at Connor's ribs. He dug his heels in, resisting. 'Not there, please, not there!'

Jarrow grinned, the stink of him adding to the smell and Connor's panic. 'Nah, not today, boy. She's got other plans for you.' He headed to a mercifully empty alcove, pulled open a low door, and pressed Connor's head down to shove him inside. 'Yes, other plans. Probably not happy ones.' He smirked, banged the door shut with a clang, twisted a key, and stamped with the key to the fire. 'Food and drink,' he shouted at Beron. 'And water for the *student.*'

Chapter Nine

Queen of the Caverns

Beauty tossed her head, snorted, and side-stepped in the air.

'Whoa, Beauty, there's a good mare.' Gwen stroked the black horse's mane. Please let them be near the Danae caverns in the Deep Forest, and please let Beauty's distress be caused by Verian's wolves. Shivering, barely able to see in the late afternoon gloom, Gwen peered through heavy wet flakes of snow drifting to the ground.

Two days from Ilatias, she had spent the first night in a barn, no sign of the farmer, his family or livestock. Rising early, trusting Beauty to find the way in the pre-dawn dark, she flew east all day with one rest. And this had been cut short when winter-hungry wolves stalked them from the trees ringing the clearing where Beauty landed. Not waiting to check how many, Gwen hauled herself on to the snorting horse and shouted, 'Fly', as the pack sprang snarling from the trees. Beauty's flailing hooves knocked one to the ground, the others jumping, jaws snapping.

Gwen didn't dare land until she could be certain it was safe.

There, beyond the familiar massive, bare oak. Relief flooded her at the sight of a ledge which fronted a cave opening into a rocky wall, home to Verian's wolves. On the ledge, two Danae guards in leather tunics and fur cloaks shaded their eyes from the glare of the setting sun to follow her progress to the ground.

Gwen waved, called, 'Maikin, well met,' and landed Beauty silently in the fresh drifts blanketing the narrow swathe of earth between the oak and the ledge.

'Gwen?' The older and stouter of the two guards jumped to the ground and shuffled forward, knee high in white powder. He carried a spear. 'What are you doing here in the middle of winter?'

'I have news, old friend, terrible news. I need your queen's help.' Gwen dismounted and hugged Maikin, who patted her awkwardly on the shoulder. 'I'll tell you everything once we're inside.' She laid a gentling hand on the nervous Beauty's nose. 'We've journeyed from the Citadel, and met with hungry wolves on our way.' She grimaced. 'Can you take us in, or do you need to stay here?'

Maikin pulled at his thick beard, the brown heavily streaked with silver to match his curling hair. 'From the Citadel? Hmm. If there's terrible news, I want to hear it with the queen.' He called to the second, much younger, guard. 'I'll send someone along, son. Keep your senses keen if there's danger about.'

'The danger I speak of isn't close,' Gwen said. 'Not yet.'

Maikin raised his heavy eyebrows. 'Come on,' he grunted.

Gwen followed the guard along a path hugging the rocky hillside to a slim opening between two high, sheer cliffs. Maikin halted, peered upwards, and waved his spear at a man standing on the cliff top.

'Send another to take my place. I'll be with Her Majesty if you need me.'

Looking over his shoulder at Gwen, Maikin strode between the cliffs. The way soon narrowed into a deeply shadowed gorge bordered with snow-laden shrubs and boulders. Away from the wolf scent, Beauty relaxed. She had visited here many times. She nudged Gwen's shoulders, her eyes bright.

'Yes, I'm sure Verian will have treats for you,' Gwen said.

Maikin disappeared into an opening in the rock face. Gwen hesitated briefly, and went in after him. While her fear of being underground had never left her, she could relax in these high, wide, and well-lit passages. In summer, when she often visited, fresh grasses and sweet herbs covered the earth floors, and giant pots filled with young trees, fruiting bushes, herbs, and wildflowers lined the walls. Moving through the caverns was close to walking along a woodland path in her own Forest at the edge of the ocean.

This was winter, and the pots bore young, red-berried holly, and pine trees which filled the air with their scent. Lanterns hung from the ceilings, casting everything in a warm, yellow light. Coal-filled bronze braziers glowed between the pots, and the heavy curtains to people's living spaces were pulled aside to let the heat of their cooking fires escape into the hallways – together with smells of herb-laden stews and soups. Gwen's stomach rumbled. She'd had nothing to eat since a hasty breakfast of bread and goat's cheese in the barn in the early morning.

The great wooden doors to the queen's throne room stood open, framing Verian, arms outstretched. Tall, slim as a young birch, her long dark hair gleamed as black as ever. Her green eyes glittered with welcome.

'Gwen, how wonderful.'

Gwen released Beauty's reins and threw herself into Verian's embrace. A rich scent of spice and herbs enfolded her. She inhaled, remembering their first meeting, twenty years past, when she and Mark followed the dour Maikin to meet the former Queen of the Caverns, Verian's aunt. Who promptly imprisoned them. All different since those times.

Maikin summoned a guard to take Beauty to the underground stall kept ready for her and Gwen's visits, along with oats and water. Gwen would check her later, glad her horse would be clean, fed, and comfortable.

'They tell me you bring bad news, and have ridden from Ilatias,' Verian said. 'Bad news indeed for you to travel in this weather.' She released Gwen and stood back, smiling her placid smile. 'Bad or not, it's good to see you, my friend.'

'And you.' Tears welled, and Gwen understood how much she was relying on her friend's help and advice.

'Come in,' Verian said. 'I've asked for food and wine in my chamber. We can talk privately there.'

Maikin coughed, and Verian spoke to the Head Guard. 'You too, of course, Maikin. It will save me repeating myself.' She smiled.

Verian set off across the throne room, rustling the sweet-smelling dry straw as she walked. A number of her subjects sat on leather cushions beneath walls which glowed with jewels heaped in carved-out alcoves. Wide-eyed with curiosity at this unseasonal visit, they gave Gwen tiny waves and whispered questions to each other. Their queen would tell them when she was ready. Patience.

'Start with the news you bring and why you were in Ilatias.' Verian pulled out a carved wooden chair for Gwen from a small, round table, took one for herself and gestured for Maikin to sit too.

Slices of steaming meat, heaped winter vegetables, bowls of fruit, and jugs of wine and water waited on the table. Gwen piled her wooden platter high, her mouth watering from the delicious scent.

'You remember Lady Melda?' she said, fork poised over her food. 'The Sleih Seer in cahoots with Lord Rafe, the Madach warlord? She planned to help him steal the Danae and sell us to rich lords and ladies as fairytales come to life.'

'Yes.' Verian forked a slice of meat and held it mid-air. 'Didn't King Ieldon take her powers from her, in Etting, when she tried to bewitch Tristan?'

'He did.' Gwen laid down her fork, her hunger gone. 'Not enough of them though.' She blinked at Verian through more tears. 'She's back, and she's stolen Connor, and Tristan's son too.'

'Connor? That charming boy?' Verian reached across and clasped Gwen's hands. 'Oh no, Gwen. We are here to help. Tell me what we must do.'

Chapter Ten

The battle for the refugees

A line of Madach from the surrounding villages straggled along the road into the Citadel, extending as far as Callie could see. They walked with bundles on their backs, hauled laden carts, or came in wagons where wide-eyed children and old people clung to boxes and sacks. Bleating goats and sheep and stolid cows were tethered behind.

The sight reminded Callie of the tales of the Danae journeying from the Sleih kingdom so many, many years ago. Like the Danae, these banished people had trudged along winter-rutted tracks in falling snow. Unlike the Danae, these people were travelling to the Citadel, not away from it, warned by Sleih couriers on flying horses to seek refuge while they could.

Not all had fled. Many farmers remained with their animals. Callie prayed to the Beings their barns and stone houses would protect them from Melda's grotesque creatures.

'I wish Elrane were here.' Princess Emeryn clasped the stone wall of the high tower's walkway, anxious eyes on Callie. 'These poor people, torn from their homes.'

Sleih guards patrolled the battlements. Callie shaded her eyes from the glare of the noon sun and searched the distant fields, northward. Asfal had gone with the Sleih soldiers on their flying horses to scout for signs of Melda's approach. Worry curdled in her gut. Three days since the scouts had left, and no word had arrived.

Callie laid her hand on the princess's arm, drawing and giving comfort. 'Elrane and Mark will come as quickly as they can. Meanwhile, King Ieldon is more than capable of defending Ilatias.'

'Yes, yes.' A reluctant smile tugged at Emeryn's lips. 'And I also understand what Elrane and his guard are doing is right and proper, except …'

'… except,' Callie went on, 'freeing the last of Lord Rafe's former empire from the remaining tyrants is taking too long.'

'Yes,' Emeryn said with the merest hint of anger. 'And by far the greatest need is here.'

Prince Elrane returned often to the Citadel and stayed for lengthy periods, not wanting to be a stranger to his wife or children, or the people who would one day be his subjects. Such a day, however, was far off, and meanwhile the soldierly prince wished to be useful. As he confessed to Callie, 'Books and study are not for me. Why should I study myself when I can call on the collective wisdom of the Seers at any time?' He had grinned. 'Given I'm a warrior with no enemy, I must learn the skills of justice and diplomacy and, as needed, warfare, wherever I find it.'

The prince had an enemy now.

They come. Is all prepared?

Asfal's voice sounded in Callie's mind. Her relief at hearing him fled at the message he sent. Her body tightened. They come.

There are refugees on the roads, she said. *How far is the enemy? How long do we have?*

Close. They will be with you by dusk. With us. I am not far from you.

'Callie?' Emeryn frowned at Callie's fingers tightening on her arm.

'The enemy will be here by dusk.' Callie released the princess's arm and walked swiftly to the tower stairs. 'I'll tell the king.'

Emeryn put her hands to her face. 'I'll make sure the Healers are prepared,' she said, 'and see what can be done to make sure everyone is inside the walls.' She cast an anxious glance at the long, trailing line of refugees before hurrying to the hospital and the Healers.

Callie took one last look too. She shared Emeryn's unspoken fear.

***

Her army of beauties spread below her, a white blanket of heaving fur, hair, and skin. Melda had released them from the caverns, greeted them as they emerged from crevasses onto the glacier, and rode triumphantly above their hurtling flight across the mountains and onto the High Plains with their scarce villages.

They swept across all with unnatural speed. Melda had nurtured their hunger for flesh and blood, starved them, baited them with visions of how they would gorge their fierce appetites at journey's end. Neither the snowdrifts piled against rocks in the mountains, nor the heavily churned mud of the fields slowed them. Her beauties.

The great spirit which she had conjured murmured its encouragements, assuring Melda her heart's desire, all she wished for, was ripe for the plucking. Her pulse thrummed with the heady delight of revenge, the knowledge she would take the idiot Ieldon's throne. The Gryphon pendant would be wrenched from that foolish girl – the witch, Jarrow called her. And afterwards … what once she had plotted to achieve using Lord Rafe's ambitions, she would be strong enough to do alone. The sweetness of power was honey on her tongue.

Her horse shied sideways, and Melda calmed the animal, which was forever uneasy in the presence of the white beasts. A lowing group of cattle bunched in a corner by a fence told her they had reached the fields where the Madach farmed. The horde passed through, barely pausing. Melda's aim was higher than cows. Besides, she wanted no delay.

She would reach the Citadel at dusk and enter by the great gates which stood open day and night. She savoured the image of her white beauties swirling up the spiralling cobbled road which led to the Tower, a mass of vengeful, famished cravings. Warm anticipation tingled in her veins.

All afternoon, Melda rode south and west, the paws and

feet of her white beauties sending pleasing waves of sound drumming in the air. As she rode, her urgency for haste grew, encouraged by a sour realisation she might be expected.

No people trod the roads between villages. No carts trundled by. No smoke curled from chimneys in the clear, cold air. In the fields, few livestock huddled together for warmth. Barn doors were shut, no farmers laboured in their farmyards, no hens scratched at icy puddles. The Madach had fled, either to the Deep Forest of Arneithe or, more likely, to the Citadel.

'Not far to go, my beauties,' Melda growled. Her horse flinched from her voice.

And there, ahead of her army, she found proof. The ragged end of a line of wagons pulled by horses or donkeys, or carts piled with treasured possessions hauled by sturdy Madach men and women. Sleih soldiers mounted on black horses barred the way between Melda's racing beasts and the carts. The blue-winged gryphon which stopped her from stealing the prince's brats flew above the soldiers.

The Sleih and Madach would resist her victorious entry. Rage blossomed in Melda's chest.

***

Callie had returned to the battlements above the gates, gazing north at the distant but fast approaching monstrous swarm. If she hadn't earlier seen these creatures for herself, she might have considered them a pretty sight with their white skin and fur tinged pink by the setting sun. A black horse flew over the horde, carrying a figure wearing a streaming cloak.

Melda.

Yes, she is here. Asfal responded to Callie's thought.

Flying a great distance ahead of the returning scouts, the gryphon hovered above the Sleih soldiers barring the monsters from the trail of refugees. Although the white mass behind them was hidden from their view, the Madach at the end of the straggling line sensed the danger at their heels. They urged their animals on, pressing those ahead, creating a crush of wagons and teetering possessions. The line came to a tangled halt.

Callie squeezed her fingers together.

We won't get everyone safely in, she called to Asfal. *They need to abandon their wagons if they're to be saved.*

A commotion caused Callie to look to the gates. As word of the attackers spread, the crowd coming in thickened, blocking horsemen attempting to leave the Citadel to help the refugees. Another crush formed. Shouts, the wails of children, braying of donkeys and whinnying horses added to the chaos.

'Calm! Let us have calm.'

King Ieldon's voice sounded above it all. Mounted on his horse on a low rise inside the wall, he raised his hands in supplication. Sleih Seers accompanied him, eyes closed in concentration. The Seers' soothing presence filled Callie's mind. The panicked people at the gates, nearer, would feel it more strongly. This was a time when Sleih powers of the mind were needed to save lives.

The crowd hushed. Donkeys and horses lowered their heads. Children ceased their crying. The refugees shuffled to the sides of the gates. The horsemen passed at a gallop. The people carried on with an orderly entry into the Citadel where Sleih waited to direct them to shelter.

The horsemen moved among the families on the road, lifting sobbing children and quaking elderly Madach from wagons and carrying them to the gates. Others unharnessed horses, boosted two or three people onto each, and slapped the horses on the rumps to send them cantering forward. Livestock were untethered, lumbering after the horses.

A small flock of sheep refused to follow. They huddled by an abandoned wagon, bleating their terror into the cloud-shadowed dusk.

Callie's anxious mind searched until she found what she needed – a fox and his vixen cowering in their den beneath a leafless hedge.

Please, she begged them. *Do what you can.*

With great reluctance, the two crawled from their shelter into the road. They herded the sheep, prodded and nipped like the most vigilant of shepherd dogs, until the animals ran, noisy with panic, to the gates.

Thank you. I owe you.

You do, came the fox's weary reply.

Callie's mind stayed with the pair until they were safely back in their den under the hedge. She would make good on her promise, somehow.

The distance to the seething mass of monsters shortened. The horde spread across the road and fields like a violent breaking wave, glowing sickly pale in the fading light.

With the last of the refugees in the care of the horsemen, the barrier of Sleih on their flying horses rose into the air to challenge the attackers. Asfal led them, his great wings beating steadily.

Callie clenched her fists to her sides, sending her magic to join with the gryphon's, strengthening his power against the evil wielded by the Seer.

***

Melda's fury burned with a fierce intensity. She would not be cheated of her victory. Pushing her nervous mount closer to the horde, she sent out a shrill, voiceless cry: *Fight, my beauties, and your rewards will be bountiful.*

Cool murmurs of encouragement sounded within her own head: *Together, we cannot be beaten. Together, we will vanquish our enemies.*

Glee laced Melda's anger. Yes, the greater power was hers.

The monsters reared up to meet the attacking Sleih.

***

The last of the refugees spilled through the gates, bumped aside by several terrified sheep.

The massive, thick wooden doors of the Citadel swung shut with a thud which echoed off the stone walls. Crafted from oak from the ancient Forest of Arneithe, these sturdy gates would withstand the most ferocious of attacks. Sleih Seers stood before them, stretching their arms to embrace the wood. They chanted magic words to infuse the gates with greater strength to resist whatever powers Melda might throw at them. The chanting floated to Callie watching from the battlement, strengthening her own courage as she watched the battle on the fields beyond the Citadel.

Fying Sleih soldiers clashed with the horde, spreading their attack along the front of the snarling, writhing mass. The creatures bared long, yellow fangs, snarling, shrieking. The soldiers swooped with raised swords to hack at white fur and skin, cutting down one monster after the other. But their efforts made a bare difference to the numbers massed on the bloodied snow.

Asfal thrust out his eagle legs to rip exposed necks and chests, circling and twisting to plunge his huge beak into matted scalps. Blood flowed from his lion sides.

The king's voice sounded in Callie's mind.

Fall back. The gates are secured.

The black horses swiftly rose high into the dark sky, their churning hooves rippling the cold air around the watchers on the walls.

Denied its enemy, the horde milled about, snapping at each other. Callie dared hope it would destroy itself, until Melda appeared. She bent close to her horse's mane, sweeping across her vile army. As she passed, they calmed, lying in the muddy snow as if to rest.

A sob went up from the watchers as two dark shapes were revealed, shadows in the white snow which gleamed in the last of the light. Not all the Sleih riders had returned.

Asfal flew low over Callie, his bloodied sides heaving.

I did not find her, he said.

'Not yet.' Callie ran to the stairs, calling in her mind for Lady Clara, the Seer Healer, to meet her in the courtyard by the stables. 'We will when the time is ripe. We will face her and defeat her together, as we did before.'

The stakes are the same.

You and I are stronger.

As is she, Asfal warned.

Chapter Eleven

A promise

'Where have you been?' Melda perched, taut as a strung bow, on a pile of white furs by a fire which blazed warmly despite its cool-looking blue and silver flames. Behind her, a pavilion had been hastily erected with wood from a nearby copse covered with the skins of those creatures slain in the brief battle. Her temper burned hotter than the fire.

'I have no flying horse like you.' Jarrow stiffly dismounted from a young bay gelding. He returned Melda's glare.

She was tempted to strike him because someone had to be struck, and the grubby captain was available. With effort, she stayed her hand. He still had his uses.

'I expected to find you enthroned in the Citadel with Ieldon and his court prostrate at your feet,' Jarrow taunted.

Melda ground her teeth. Idiot. He had grown too used to her powerless ways in the early years they travelled together, and was too stupid to understand all had changed. She smiled inwardly. He would learn, in time.

'Spies,' she said. 'Ieldon expected us.'

Jarrow eased himself onto a log which served as a seat by the fire. He stretched his hands to the warmth. 'What next?'

'There are ways to make them submit without doing battle.' Melda stirred the silver-glowing coals with a stick. Flames erupted in a firework of dancing blue and white sparks. 'But while I am busy here, there are the Danae to deal with.'

'Yes.' Jarrow set his palms on his knees. 'You promised me my fairytale slaves.'

'I did. And you can have them.'

'How? I can't march in there by myself and throw them all into chains.' He waved at the sleeping white army. 'And this lot will eat them. No good to me eaten.'

Melda narrowed her eyes. 'If you are willing to share – and there are enough for sharing – I will give you help to seize them.' She poked at the fire, remembering other beautiful blue and white flames. The Madach robber tents burning as punishment for their stupidity, their inability to find and keep imprisoned two Danae children. Children! She was pleased she had restrained herself, had left the clumsy idiots alive and with minds more or less intact. They would finally pay their debt to her. Under Jarrow's heavy hand, even that ragged band might be capable of capturing the defenceless Danae.

'There is one I want for myself,' she said. 'The enchanted golden-haired beauty, Lucy, mother to one of our guests in the caverns.'

'Another hostage.' Jarrow nodded his approval.

'One who has the brat prince's affection, sister to the witch.' She gave a grim smile. 'A worthy hostage.'

'Anything to upset the witch.' Jarrow's eyes glinted.

'Tomorrow I will search out your new allies,' Melda said. 'They have modest ambitions. The bulk of the riches will be yours.' She stood and walked around the fire to peer deeply into Jarrow's eyes. 'To ensure victory, and to keep your allies true, I will send a pack of my beauties with you to the Danae.' She stalked back to her furs, saying, 'The power I imbued in you means the creatures will obey you. Use my army wisely.'

***

In the besieged Citadel, Willow lay in bed. She stared at the moonlit ceiling, mulling over what she'd learned about this Lady Melda. A once-upon-a-time Seer of the Sleih and a member of Grandfather's trusted Council, now a traitor who had joined somehow with an Evil dwelling in the High Alps of Asfarlon. If Callie's Gryphon pendant fell into the lady's hands, it would be catastrophic. Melda had stolen Callie's nephew and the son of Callie's friend as hostages. Her heart ached at the thought of the two, imprisoned in a dark cave by a wicked woman who had no care whether they lived or died once she used them to get what she wanted.

Willow understood the problem in rescuing the boys. Callie's proof they were in the caverns of the High Alps had come at the near cost of her life, despite being protected by magic and Asfal. Anyone approaching the caverns with strong powers would easily be detected and attacked, driven away like Callie. Anyone without Sleih powers or magic would be helpless against the lady and her horrific beasts.

However ... Willow sat up in bed and stared through her window. The clouds of dusk had been driven away by the wind, and stars gleamed sharp-edged as diamonds. What if the rescuer didn't have enough magic to easily provoke the beasts, but enough to escape should they need to? A rescuer like ... herself.

Hadn't Grandfather said, 'You resisted her well, no mean feat?'

Willow excelled in her lessons and had listened closely to the tales of the Old Sleih. The caverns of Asfarlon were by a glacier. She was sure she could find her way there and ... she would work the rest out when she found the glacier.

She would leave tonight, while the palace slept.

Slipping out of bed, Willow dressed in heavy boots, thick leggings and tunic, with a woollen coat over those. She laid her warmest cloak and hat on her bed, and grabbed a bag to carry the remains of her supper, sitting under covers on a table by the window. She considered whether she should leave a message for her mother, to say she hadn't been stolen like the others.

'Willow, psst, are you awake?'

Rowan's head came around the door, followed by the rest of him when he saw her out of bed and dressed.

'What's going on?' he said.

'Why are you here?' Willow threw out her free hand. 'You should be asleep.'

Rowan snorted. 'So should you.' He glanced at the cloak

on the bed, and at the bag Willow held open as she tipped in bread rolls and a wedge of cheese.

'Not the right time for a picnic, Sis.' He waved at the window. 'Being dark and freezing cold aren't the only reasons it's a bad idea to go out there.'

Willow groaned. 'Not funny.' She hesitated, before confessing, 'I'm going to fly there on Dreamer, find Connor and the other boy, rescue them.' She stared at her brother, waiting for his teasing mockery.

'Uh, uh.' He took a step into the room. 'Kez and me are coming too.'

'You are?' Willow reached for the small tinder box and candles which sat on the fireplace mantel.

'Yes. It's why I came. I figured it like this–'

'–just enough magic?'

Rowan laughed. 'We read other other's minds, even without Sleih powers.'

'Mother will worry,' Willow said.

'Callie will understand. She'll make Mother understand it's for the best.'

Rowan didn't sound convinced. Would Callie be on their side and persuade their mother not to take soldiers from the defence of Ilatias to chase after them? Grandfather might understand better than Mother. Perhaps he would convince her. Willow huffed. Too many hopes and perhapses.

'Dress warmly and meet me at the stables,' she said. 'We'll use the tunnel. Melda's scouts, if she has them, won't see us leaving and she won't try to kidnap us again.'

Rowan slipped out the door. Willow tossed the last of her supper into the bag. Her pulse pounded, both with fear at their audacity and the thrill of doing something.

She crept her way to the stables, sending ahead tiny probing thoughts to find out where guards or servants might be. The servants slept. There were no guards – those not resting were on the walls, watching the enemy.

Willow? Shouldn't you be in bed?

Willow startled. She had forgotten Asfal, recovering from

his wounds in his huge stall with its double doors opening onto the stable yard. He preferred the freedom of the air, the forest and the mountains, and rarely used the stall. Nevertheless, the Master of Horse made sure there was always a fresh bed of meadow hay or straw for him.

Willow held her bag close to her chest.

Rowan's coming too. We're going to rescue Connor and the other boy. She tried to make the statement sound normal, like rescuing the boys was what they would, should, be doing.

Ah. I see. A pause. *And will I need to rescue you and Rowan a second time?*

I hope not. Willow tiptoed into the dark stall and whispered, 'We have the best chance of not being spotted too early, and Grandfather said I resisted that woman well, so I thought ...'

You can sneak in and out with no one the wiser?

'Yes. Especially as she's here, so we likely won't come across her at all.' Willow hoped.

Asfal's breath warmed her cheek. 'Are you telling Callie?' she asked when he didn't reply. Her stomach sank.

No. A longer pause. *The Healer tells me I cannot fight in further battles until these scratches fully heal.* He blinked rapidly. *Healers have no understanding of how quickly gryphons recover.*

'Willow, where are you?'

She jumped at Rowan's loud whisper. 'With Asfal.'

'Oh.' Rowan stood in the doorway, his silhouette dark against the starlit night. 'Is he telling Callie?'

The gryphon's head brushed Willow's hair. *I am coming with you,* he said. *It will save me the bother of rescuing you later. Besides, it will be quicker if you both ride on me, and safer for Kez and Dreamer.*

Willow's heart leapt, before she cautioned, 'There'll be four of us.' If they were lucky. 'Can you carry us all?'

Humph.

Willow dared put her arms around the gryphon's feathery neck. 'If we go by the tunnel, her scouts won't see us.' She giggled. 'I think you'll fit. The horses do.'

No. I will fly, and make sure I'm seen. Then I will rise high before meeting you where the tunnel exits above the river.

'Good idea,' Rowan said. 'Lady Melda will believe you're here, guarding and watching. Makes sense.' He touched Willow's arm. 'Come on, let's go before anyone discovers us.'

Rowan led their way across the stable yard. Cautiously opening a squeaky gate into a winter-bare orchard, he carried on beyond the frost-glistening trees to a high stone wall bordering the kitchen gardens. A rusty iron ring was nailed into the stones at about the height of his waist. Rowan twisted it, whispering the words he had learned when he was old enough to be trusted with this carefully held royal secret. A pair of wooden gates shimmered into place. Rowan pushed one gate open, and ushered Willow in. Rather than coming out in the formal gardens beyond, another wall faced them. Between the two, a steep rough path ran into blackness.

Willow stepped in front of Rowan. She cupped her hands, murmured a few words in Old Sleih. A soft white light glowed through her fingers like an old-fashioned glowstone. 'Let's go.' She hefted her bag over her shoulder.

Chapter Twelve

The Blue Lady returns

Goosebumps ran up Isa's arms. The coldness which flowed in her veins was nothing to do with the freezing pre-dawn air. She straightened from crouching over the fire in the centre of the camp, where she and two other women fed the flames. A pot of bubbling porridge hung on a large iron tripod. Behind a roughly made fence at the edge of the leafless trees, horses stamped their hooves, their low snorts misting the air. No one else was about. The rest of the Madach robbers huddled under furs in their tents, their dogs adding to the stuffy warmth inside.

Contrary to the coldness, the skin of Isa's throat tingled with a gentle heat. Frowning, she reached under her cloak and inside her dress to lift out the ring she wore on a chain around her neck. The green emerald in its delicate silver mounting had darkened. The silver circle glowed. Without thinking why, Isa unhooked the clasp and slipped the ring on her middle finger. It fitted perfectly.

This was the ring the king of the Sleih gave Isa twenty years ago. It was a thank-you gift for warning him the Madach robbers planned to steal the Danae from his small group of travellers in the depths of the Deep Forest. Isa didn't want the Danae girl, Gwen, sold as a fairytale slave, for Gwen had promised to be friends with the lonely Isa. Treasured and kept hidden from the greedier of the other Madach, the ring had never shown any sign of being anything except a ring. This morning, the smooth silver tickled her finger like the wings of a trapped moth.

Isa glanced at her helpers, berating herself for showing the jewel like this. She needn't have worried – the two women were motionless. One was stilled in the act of throwing wood on the fire, the other stirring the porridge.

Isa gasped. Old, unwanted memories sprang alive. She whirled about, and stared.

A lady rode into the camp, relaxed and confident as if she owned it all. She halted her black horse at the edge of the firelight and gazed slowly around, ignoring Isa and the women.

The Blue Lady.

Isa's heart pumped hard. Instinctively, she clasped her hands together inside her cloak, wanting for some reason to hide the ring. Motionless like her companions, she pretended to stare stupidly while taking in this unexpected and unwelcome arrival.

The lady's beauty had not faded. Her smooth, honey-coloured skin bore no signs of age, although her hair was white, glistening in coiled braids pinned with blue gems in silver clasps. She held herself tall in her saddle, her rich blue cloak with its silver trim falling over the flanks of her high-stepping black horse with its delicate painted hoofs. Her tall boots shone, bearing no sign of travel.

Isa had once badly coveted those boots. Not an envious thought entered her head this morning. Hatred at how the lady had burned Isa and her da's tent, at how she fuddled the minds of the strongest of the robbers, including their leader, Chester, welled inside her. Isa fought the urge to scream, to wake the camp and send the lady packing. It would need more than screaming to get rid of her, though. Isa waited, the ring's warmth on her finger soothing her roiling emotions.

'You.' The lady pointed with a gloved hand. 'Who's in charge of this rabble these days?'

Isa lifted her chin. 'Me.'

The lady narrowed her eyes. Twin lines creased her smooth forehead. 'Where are the men?'

Isa bristled. Then the memory surfaced of how the lady probed Chester's mind and read everything there. She clenched her fingers around the ring and calmed her thoughts. If it would do any good.

The lady, however, had no interest in whatever was in Isa's head. Remaining on her horse, she gazed around at the shabby, rain-stained tents scattered haphazardly on the trodden, muddy snow, and at the piles of rubbish littering the clearing. She smirked.

Isa didn't move her head, pretending disinterest in this inspection.

'It seems,' the Blue Lady said with a hint of teasing fun, 'your leadership hasn't brought wealth and good living, my dear.'

Isa bit her tongue, galled the lady made fun of their poor existence. She let her gaze drop and her jaw slacken, as happened to poor Chester.

The lady smiled graciously, like one about to bestow a great favour. 'I can change it all,' she said, kindly. 'You recall, I'm sure, how the men here were obsessed with finding the Danae brats they lost – three times.' She gave a tinkling laugh, like the loss of the Danae amused her.

Isa recalled. Especially, she recalled the Blue Lady's utter fury at the failure of the robbers' raid on the king's companions. Isa witnessed, horrified, the lady's blue and silver fiery revenge on the Madach robbers' tents. She kept her gaze on the ground and her hands clasped, a picture of stupid obedience. She was glad of the touch of the ring against her fingers.

The Blue Lady didn't wait for an answer. 'I will give you your Danae,' she said, 'your fairytale slaves. More than you can deal with.'

Her silky voice flowed through Isa. A desire to enfold it, keep it, obey whatever command the lady might give, tugged at her. The ring fluttered, an urgent pulsing which spread through Isa's body. Her mind cleared. She would not obey this wicked woman.

The hooves of the Blue Lady's horse sucked at the dirty slush in front of Isa. She steeled herself, wary of this closer contact. The lady bent, lifted Isa's chin. Her green eyes raked her face as if she would count every freckle. Isa let her mouth drop open, and her eyelids half-close.

'I will send you a soldier,' the lady purred. 'A man who has dealt with these Danae in the past. He will lead your fighting men to them, and you will take them.'

Isa worried the lady must hear the loud drumming of her heart. The ring's fluttering slowed to a gentle soothing. Stay calm.

'His name is Jarrow,' the Blue Lady said, 'and you will do what he tells you.' She squeezed Isa's chin, let it drop. 'You, and he, will have your riches.' She favoured Isa with a conspiratorial grin. 'There is one marked for me. One alone. I will have the golden-haired beauty. And vengeance.'

With no further word, she wheeled the horse about, shook the reins, and cantered from the camp.

Isa stared after her, her fingers twisting the cooled ring.

The younger of the women, able to move, yanked Isa's arm. 'Who was that?' she asked, awe in her voice. 'And what was she talking about? Everyone knows Danae aren't real.'

'Not everyone,' Isa said. She turned away to thread the ring on its chain before picking up a log to throw on the leaping fire. Her thoughts went to her friend Gwen, and how they had met when Gwen and her brother were captured by Isa's da and her Uncle Viv. Although Isa had been given the task of making sure Gwen didn't escape, somehow, in a very short time, they had become friends, and Isa had secretly helped the brother and sister more than once. And there was Gwen's sister too, the kind and beautiful Lucy with her golden hair, so different from Isa's own tangled auburn locks. When Lucy had allowed Isa to stroke her hair, it was like stroking a kitten. Isa smiled wistfully at the memory as she returned to feeding the fire.

If what the Blue Lady said was true, the Danae brother and sisters – grown men and women now, like Isa – needed her help once more. She reached under her cloak and rubbed the king's ring. Somehow, Isa would save the family again.

Chapter Thirteen

Ancient Asfarlon

Willow crouched against Asfal's silky feathers, Rowan pressed behind her. Whiteness blinded her, swirling gusts of snow whipped about by a freezing, howling wind. She shivered inside her cloak. She and Rowan, flying on Dancer and Kez, would never have survived this horrendous journey by themselves.

They had left Ilatias in starlit darkness and flown north over the lightless High Plains as the moon set to their left. When day came, gathering clouds obscured the low winter sun, made worse by the blizzard.

The weather alone wasn't responsible for the dusk-like gloom. The closer they came to the High Alps, the more uneasy Willow became. An awful presence hovered in the air, dark and evil. She cringed at the sense of flying into an oily cobweb which left sticky dabs on her cloak and gloves. It must be the Evil which Grandfather spoke of when Willow overheard the grownups talking. The one Melda had, or might have, joined with. Would this Evil sense Asfal? Or her?

'Do you feel it?' a voice murmured into her hair.

Rowan's voice, yet not his. Slow, thick. Willow twisted her head to the side. 'Yes,' she shouted, her voice carried away by the wind. 'It's the Evil.'

Rowan giggled. Willow's skin crawled. 'No,' she cried. 'It's not funny. Resist it, Rowan, try!'

'Resist? Why resist?' The voice echoed, as if coming from a great depth.

'Asfal.' Willow tugged on the gryphon's feathers. *Asfal, something bad's happening to Rowan. We have to get out of here.*

There is wickedness in this blizzard, Asfal said. *Do we turn back?*

Willow squinted at the oily snow coating her gloves, making it difficult to keep a hold on Asfal's feathers. She kept her face down, dreading the sticky droplets touching her skin. She wanted to flee, while they still could.

It would mean leaving the boys to Melda's mercies. Rowan or strangers? Lady Melda triumphant? Willow battled the desperate desire to save Rowan first.

Can we escape from this blizzard? Quickly?

'Our hearts' desires, if we give ourselves …'

The dark, deep voice coming from her brother stabbed at Willow's mind. She concentrated on Asfal's neck, held tight. Rowan's arms loosened their grip around Willow's waist. He would fall. She trembled in panic.

'No, Rowan, no. Hold tight to me, we're getting out of here.' The wind swept Willow's pleas into the storm.

Asfal, get us out of this. Anywhere. Please.

Asfal slowed, lowering his head to scan the valleys and mountains. Willow trusted his eagle eyes saw more than she did.

We will circle the mountain, find shelter at the higher levels. The Evil lurks in the lowest depths.

'Our hearts' desires. Think on that and crave it …' Rowan held his arm out, giggling.

'Now, Asfal, now,' Willow screamed into the gryphon's feathers.

Asfal tilted. Rowan slid, tipped sideways. Terrified, Willow gripped her brother's cloak and held fast. Her other hand clutched blue feathers. She prayed everything held.

The blizzard whipped at her. Rowan sniggered in her ear, chanting about hearts' desires. The voice tapped at her mind too, insistent. Willow focused on Asfal's circling flight, resisting, hard.

At last, at last, the beat of the gryphon's wings slowed. The howling wind eased. They had circled the mountain.

Rowan wriggled closer to Willow. He grabbed her waist with both hands. The treacherous voice fell silent and Willow let out a ragged breath.

Asfal stretched his legs to land on a ledge where snow covered the remains of a weathered, low stone balustrade. He didn't stop there, moving into a high cave where the wind's fury could not follow them.

Grateful for the silence, for escape from the oily, sticky blizzard, Willow slipped off the gryphon and grabbed at Rowan. He slid to the floor and sat on the cold stone with his back to Asfal's lion leg and his eyes shut.

'What happened,' he murmured. 'Did I fall asleep?'

Willow rejoiced at the normalcy of his question, asked in his own voice.

'There's evil in the air above the valleys,' she said. 'It tried to take you over, like when Lady Melda attacked us.'

'Evil?' Rowan heaved himself to his feet, planting his legs apart to steady himself. The sword at his side swung slightly, as if agitated.

An old, old, enemy of both Gryphon and Sleih,' Asfal said. *'Calllie told me the tale long ago when we both believed it belonged more to legend than history.*

'Grandfather believes it's true,' Willow said. 'It's why the Gryphon pendant was forged, to defeat the Evil.'

Yes. Aeons ago.

'Hmm.' Rowan touched the sword hilt. 'I should have drawn Celeste, that would have kept the Evil at bay.'

'Maybe.' Willow was unsure any strength remained in the sword's magic. If they'd had time, and permission, they could have asked the Seers to whisper spells over it. They had neither.

Rowan moved away from Asfal to explore the cave. Willow eyed him for any sign of strangeness. He seemed to be his old self, and she allowed herself to examine the cave too. The light from the opening extended a short distance in, enough to see this must once have been a room where someone lived. Tall bookshelves were carved into the walls, and a low stone table – of a perfect height for a gryphon to dine – sat near a large bowl sunk into the rubble-strewn floor.

A firepit, Asfal said.

'Over here.' Rowan gestured at the remains of a wooden

platform, charred and crumbling along one side. Made of oak and tucked into a corner out of the weather, it had survived the centuries well.

'Don't touch it,' Willow said. 'It'll fall to pieces.'

The charring interested her, and having spotted it on the platform, she became aware of dark scorch marks scarring the stone either side of an opening opposite the ledge.

'There was a fire,' she said, pointing to the black streaks.

Yes, like Callie told you, Asfarlon burned in the final battle against the evil. It's why the Gryphon no longer live here.

'No longer?' Rowan's voice rose a pitch in his excitement. 'You mean, there are other gryphons, and they live somewhere?'

'Really?' Willow shared her brother's eagerness to learn more. Asfal, however, shook out his wings and moved to the stone-littered firepit.

I believe the scorch marks are your path to the lower caverns, he said. *To finding Melda's hostages.*

'Your path?' Willow's brief excitement fled. 'Aren't you coming too?'

I cannot, for the Evil which exists here will see me, and be prepared. Remember your own plan, Willow. Not quite enough magic ...

'Yes, I see ...' Willow trailed off. Asfal was right, which didn't stop her heart beating harder.

'At least Lady Melda isn't here,' Rowan said, 'which gives us a better chance.'

The afternoon is late, none of us have slept or eaten. Asfal settled on the rock floor and folded his wings. *We should rest. Rowan needs to recover fully. You, Willow, will need to be alert and strong.*

Willow nodded. Resting would either calm her nerves or let her worries grow.

'We do need to eat,' she said. Doing something practical would help. She swallowed her fear, unslung from her shoulder the bag where she had stowed the rolls, cheese, and two leather water flasks.

She and Rowan ate in silence before curling inside their cloaks. Her body exhausted, Willow slept. But her restless dreams were besieged with whispering demons summoning her to join them, to achieve her heart's desire … and another, gentler murmur in a voice she did not recognise yet trusted, calling on her to have courage. Courage. Did she have enough?

Chapter Fourteen

Old history

Connor huddled in a corner of the cage, tugging tightly at the grubby fur Beron gave him the first night he was there. Along with cold and hunger, the stiff collar Jarrow forced him to wear meant he had barely slept since he'd been in the cage. He had given up his furtive attempts to unbuckle it when the leather stiffened even more, leaving him choking for air.

The tiny sharp studs pricked constantly at his skin, creating a chafing itch slightly relieved by pulling at the leather with his fingers. Sunk in misery, beginning to believe this had always been his life, Connor's memories of the Forest and his parents were splintering like a cracked mirror.

He stared between the bars at Beron, frustrated, sympathy fighting anger. The younger boy sat rigid on a stone, vacantly staring into the diminishing flames of the fire, wrapped in his own wretchedness.

Earlier, while Connor dozed, the lady and Jarrow left the cave, taking with them the grossly misshapen beasts held captive in the alcoves. The silence, broken by Beron's quiet sobbing, woke Connor. He had groaned, wanting to recapture the oblivion of sleep. Until he realised what the silence meant. He had crawled to the bars.

'Beron,' he called with cracked, dry lips. 'Beron, have they gone?'

Beron glanced Connor's way through his tears, before swinging his head to indicate the black opening leading out of the cave. The wraiths hovered at the base of the steps, their white gowns trailing the stony floor. They appeared to be asleep, if wraiths slept.

'Open this door, Beron,' Connor whispered. 'Let me out.'

Beron had shrunk into himself, shaking his head. The tall wraith, the one Jarrow called Seer Olban, opened his black eyes. He shot Beron a glare. The boy shrieked and cupped his head in his hands. Connor steeled himself for his own agony. It came, sharp as a dagger thrust. Despite his misery, sudden fury boiled inside him. Mentally, not knowing how he did it, he twisted the knife-like pain about and sent it back where it came from.

Olban jolted, and, somehow, he was beside the bars. Connor waited for the pain. It didn't come. Instead, the wraith stretched out a clawed hand towards Connor.

'The student is strong, after all.' His oily voice sent shivers tingling along Connor's spine. 'The lady has better material to work with than she knows.' And he was gone, hovering in the doorway in some ghoulish pretence of sleep.

Since then, Connor's whispered promises of freedom if Beron opened the cage couldn't persuade the traumatised boy to budge from the fire. Hence Connor's frustration. He wanted to try to escape, even though he'd probably not make it past the wraiths. Anything was better than sitting here until the lady and Jarrow returned, with or without her monsters.

He rested against the ice-cold stone, the collar's studs nipping his throat, closed his eyes, and gathered the broken fragments of his memories of home. Tears welled with a longing to be settled in his oak, gazing out at the silver-edged surf breaking on the brown cliffs around the cove. He would welcome being teased, if it meant being with his ma and his da.

Alongside his sadness, a determination to not let the lady and Jarrow win, to resist and resist and resist, formed stone-like in Connor's stomach. He shifted on the hard floor. No giving up, however many collars they wrapped around his neck, or cages they locked him in. Somehow, he would free himself and Beron. Somehow …

A sense in the change of light made him open his eyes. A pale glow shone in the dark archway to the stairs, behind the wraiths. Connor's stomach sank, taking with it his stone of resolve. She had returned. His chance was lost.

***

The stairs circled and circled, down, ever down. The pale light Willow conjured in her cupped hands floated above her shoulder, throwing shadows on the stones ahead. The solid weight of the bag on her back comforted her.

She and Rowan had left Asfal circling the mountain top to watch for Lady Melda's return while they searched for the prisoners. Their way followed twisting, scorched passages with stony floors trodden smooth by countless feet – and claws and pads. Willow hurried past dark doorways where the skitter of toenails on stone told her others had taken over the deserted spaces. Twice, she caught sight of the flick of a skinny tail scrabbling out of the light. She shuddered.

Courage.

The soothing murmur she had heard in her dreams came to her, and with it Willow saw these halls as they once must have been. Light-filled, lamps glowing yellow, Sleih and gryphons walking, talking, going about their lives. A gentle heat washed over her as it would have done when the caverns were warmed by blazing fires, sweet-scented beds were piled with furs, and the rock walls covered with paintings, books, and intricate metalwork studded with jewels mined from deep below.

Courage, I am with you.

Who was this quiet spirit? Willow stopped, pressed a hand to the cold stone. She thought of the young 'prentice Seer Callie had told her about, who battled the Evil here. 'Ilesse?' she whispered, 'are you here?'

'Who are you talking to?' Rowan frowned. 'We need to keep moving.' He shuddered. 'This place is full of ghosts.'

'Yes.' Willow smiled. 'It's good, isn't it?'

Rowan rolled his eyes and waved her on.

The floors became rougher, the stairs steeper. There were no more side tunnels, and the cobwebbed passages narrowed. The spirit – whether it was Ilesse or not – led Willow deeper into the caverns. The homely visions faded into a dank reality.

The deeper they went, the more musty and stale the air became, and the more heavily scorched the walls and floor. Willow took shallow breaths and stole quick looks behind her to make sure Rowan kept close.

She had no idea how long they had been walking when they came to a dark, steep opening with worn runes carved into the rock above. The fires which had made the caverns uninhabitable must have burned fiercest here, for the stones were charred a solid black. Slime-streaked rivulets of water ran like black poison down the walls to form stale, foul-smelling pools in the hollows of the floor. Beyond the cold damp and the sodden, charred mess of the walls, another scent lingered. Oily, ashy – like the murky fog which had hindered their flight to the Alps.

Willow's stomach tightened. They must be close to where the Evil dwelled, which meant close to the prisoners. The comforting spirit no longer travelled with her, and her fear rose with its absence. She stamped the fear down. She must have courage.

'See this?' Rowan moved to the edge of the circle of light to touch a rusted stub – the remnants of an iron bolt. 'There was a gate here once.'

'The runes are in Old Sleih.' Willow pointed above the opening. 'I'm not sure. I think it says something about treasure.'

'You think they kept treasure there?'

'Long gone, I suspect.' Willow nodded at the gaping arch. 'We need to go through there.'

Rowan stepped to the opening, his hand on Celeste's hilt. 'I wish I could go first,' he muttered. 'There's danger. I can feel it.'

Willow felt the danger too. 'It's where the boys are, I'm certain.' With the light showing the way, she pushed past her brother and stepped cautiously onto the narrow, winding, uneven steps. The tightening in her stomach grew stronger.

***

Connor squinted in the gloom. The pale light descended the stairs too slowly to be Lady Melda, and too quietly to be the stomping Jarrow. The person carrying it apparently didn't wish to be noticed, which might have worked if the cave was ablaze with fire glow and the torches on the walls had been alight.

'Beron,' he hissed. 'Someone's coming. Do you see the light?'

Beron rocked silently on the stone, unresponsive. Connor's sad frustration grew. Either the boy didn't hear, or he was too far gone in his mind to take any notice of what was happening.

The light dimmed, stopped moving. Friend or enemy? What could he lose?

'This way,' Connor called, hearing the croaking harshness of his voice. 'Help us, please help us.'

The pale glow expanded, and a dark-haired girl with a leather bag over her shoulder stepped down from the last stair into the cavern. A boy stood close at her side, his hand on a sword hilt. Connor's mouth fell open. Who? And how?

'Connor? Beron?' the girl called into the semi-darkness. The glowing orb which floated at her shoulder brightened, filling the cave with white light.

'Here. In the cage.' Heart leaping at the chance of rescue, Connor banged his cold hands on the bars. Had he met her before? 'Beron's by the fire. He needs help. He's bad.'

'Not as bad as you will be, student.'

The sneering warning came from the wraith, Olban. He drifted by the low door to the cage while his disciples formed a shimmering barrier across the archway to the stairs, blocking the boy and girl from entering.

'Let us enter.' The girl stood straight, arms at her sides, glaring at the wraiths, murmuring quickly in a language Connor didn't understand.

Connor recognised her now, although it had been four years since they met. The Sleih princess, Willow. What was she doing here?

The boy – he must be her brother, the prince – stepped in

front of the princess. He pulled the sword from its scabbard and raised it high. The glow from the hilt lit his fingers, the edges of the sword glinted.

The wraiths squirmed, fell back.

'Stay,' Olban commanded them.

The panicked wraiths coiled around each other, torn between their master and the sword.

Except for one, who must have been a giant of a man in life. Rather than fleeing the sword, he took a great stride forward and knelt before the prince.

'I am with Celeste.' His voice boomed from the cave's roof to echo in Connor's ears.

The prince – Connor was sure his name wasn't Celeste – grinned. 'Welcome,' he said, and faced the remaining wraiths with the gleaming sword upright.

The princess kept her focused pose.

'No!' Olban shrieked at the wraiths. 'Stay firm, I command you.'

Whether it was the sword or what the princess murmured or both, the wraiths let out a long, chilling moan. They cowered in a tangled heap between the prince and Olban, who was no longer by the cage. He floated before the girl, out of reach of the sword.

'My dear Ilesse,' he hissed. 'We are to be together at last? It has been too long. I have missed our conversations.'

Willow opened her eyes. 'I am not Ilesse.'

Olban did not address her, however. He stared at a spot to Willow's left. He ignored the princess's interruption. 'Surely you must understand how both your blood and your spirit, my beloved Ilesse, live on in our Lady Melda.' He smirked. 'Melda is stronger than you ever were, and has welcomed me. Soon I will cast off this dull, old shape and take a form in her.' He lifted his shoulders, loomed over the space next to Willow. The princess took a step back. 'And, my little Seer, you will at last belong to me.'

Whoever Ilesse was, Connor grew cold imagining the arrogant, vengeful lady becoming one with whatever drove this wraith.

Willow met Olban's contempt. 'She will never belong to you, Evil,' she said.

Olban scowled. 'First, the easy prey.' That smirk again.

Willow drew herself up, shut her eyes. Her lips moved. Olban reached out translucent, skinny arms to her. He tried to snatch her to him, his mouth twisting in a perverted, strangled chant.

The prince brandished the sword, protecting his sister. The long blade glowed, quivering as it strove to meet the wraith's attack.

A battle of power. From behind bars, Connor gazed anxiously from Willow to Olban, to the prince and the trembling sword.

If Olban won, they would all be imprisoned, at the mercy of the lady and Jarrow. The notion made a mockery of his hope of rescue and deepened his despair.

A stabbing pain pierced Connor's head. He gasped.

Help me, Connor. Willow's voice, firm, insistent. *Join your magic to mine.*

Join his magic? What magic? How—?

Battle this loathsome evil with me. Have courage.

Courage. Like the spark which lit inside him, a golden glow, when Jarrow imprisoned him. Like his anger at the wraith's attack and his determination to see daylight, and home. Connor searched deep inside himself, frantic, not knowing what it was he sought, how to draw courage at will. He sensed Willow's strength waver in the face of Olban's onslaught. Where was his own strength, this magic he supposedly possessed? He must find it, he must.

A second stab of pain, sharper. *Leave this to me, student,* Olban snarled in Connor's head. *This is no place for pathetic chivalry.*

No! Connor couldn't let the wraith win. He dug deep, desperate.

And found it. Not an explosion, simply a golden warmth spreading in his veins, as reassuring as the glow of a lantern-lit window at winter dusk. It eased his fear.

He reached out to Willow with his mind, and through her,

into Olban's black, soulless eyes. Together, they struggled.

The sword, Connor urged, sensing its warm, vibrating presence.

'Celeste,' Willow murmured.

The prince lifted the glowing sword, slowly, as if its weight was too much for him. Olban flicked a skeletal hand towards the weapon. Rowan faltered, grunted. Connor shifted his mind to the sword, willing it power. He felt Willow do the same.

The prince raised the sword and this time it came swiftly, easily. He plunged it into Olban's wraith. The effort sent the boy reeling backwards. The giant caught him, steadied him.

Shrieking, Olban spiralled into a black, smoky column. With the screams reaching a crescendo, the spiral collapsed into itself, disappeared. An acrid smell of oily ash hung in the air.

A dizzy calm, like stepping out of a storm into shelter, suffused Connor's body. He fell against the bars, grasping them to save himself from falling. He wanted to be sick.

Willow opened her eyes. She bent over, holding her sides and taking deep gulping breaths.

'Are you okay?' Her brother, released from the giant's supporting embrace, rested an arm shakily across his sister's shoulders. His voice trembled.

Willow straightened. The gloom and the distance across the cave didn't hide the paleness beneath her honey-coloured skin or the damp threads of her hair.

'Thank you, Connor.' Willow walked on unsteady legs to the cage, stumbling over the edges of a pile of fossilised bones where the wraiths had cowered. She tugged at the lock, saying, 'I suspected you had it, when we met the first time, but I wasn't sure.' She gave a wan smile. 'I'm glad I was right.'

Connor's attempt at a return smile failed. His legs gave way, and he slid to the ground.

'Connor?' Willow gestured to her brother. 'Use the sword,' she said.

The prince lifted the sword and poked the tip into the lock. Door and cage disintegrated into ashes, the lock into a molten pile.

'It seems Celeste keeps its magic still.' The prince returned the dulled sword to its scabbard.

Connor's dry throat burned behind the pricking collar. 'Water?' he gasped.

Willow ran to the bag lying by the stairs, pulled out a leather flask, unstoppered it, and handed it to Connor. Water had never tasted so wonderful. He forced himself not to drink it all. Willow took the flask from him, sealed it, and set it on the ground while she helped Connor to stand.

'Rowan.' Willow gently touched the collar. 'Can Celeste destroy this too?'

Of course. Rowan was the prince. Celeste must be the sword. The hope which leaped in Connor at being free of the choking collar died when the prince shook his head.

'I daren't.' He chewed his lip. 'What if it hurts Connor? I can't control how much magic it uses. I'm sorry.'

'It's okay.' Connor slid his disappointment under the greater mound of his gratitude. 'However you got here, I'm truly, truly grateful for freeing me.' He supported himself with a hand pressed to the rock face, his legs less shaky. 'And if we want to stay free, we need to get out of here before Lady Melda comes back.'

'The lady is busy besieging Ilatias, which gives us time,' Willow said, frowning into Connor's face, checking he was all right. 'Where's the other one, Beron?'

The stone where Beron had sat by the fire was empty. Connor bit his lip. His nausea had faded and his dizziness gone. Siege or not, Jarrow might come shouting and stamping into the cave, and Connor would rather not be here when he did.

'Beron?' he called.

'There.' The prince pointed to a far alcove where a shape huddled between two rocks, its shoulders heaving.

Willow reached the boy before Connor did. She squatted beside him. 'It's over, Beron. I'm Willow, and this is Rowan, and we've come to take you home.'

Beron lifted a tear-stained face to her soothing voice. Willow gazed into his eyes for a long time. Finally, she blinked, and took him in her arms.

'He's too hurt for me to fix. He needs Callie, or Grandfather. Poor, poor boy.'

'He can walk though?' the prince said.

'Yes, he can walk.' Willow stood and raised Beron by lifting him under his arms. He came to her shoulder. 'If you take one side, Rowan, and you the other, Connor, if you're strong enough yourself, we can walk him out of here.'

'I will carry the lad.'

The giant's booming tone startled them all. Connor had forgotten him. He blinked.

'You're a real flesh-and-blood person.' Connor eyed the solid form of a tall, broad Sleih whose muscles suggested he worked hard physically in his life.

'I am.' The giant lifted his shoulders as if testing he could control them. 'Your Highness,' he said, kneeling again to the prince. 'I'm your humble subject, Thrak the miner.' He stared up, frowning. 'You carry Celeste, therefore you are heir to the Sleih. Yet you are not my prince, Varane. How much time has passed since I entered the tunnels with Olban and his companions?'

'Thrak. Oh.' Willow ran her gaze over the miner as if she had stumbled across a legendary beast. 'A very long time,' she said. 'I'll tell you once we're out of here.' She glanced at the dark stairway.

'The way you came,' Connor said, his mind clearing, 'is the way the lady uses. We might bump right into her if we go up those stairs.'

'There are other ways, if you will follow me.' Thrak bent and lifted Beron, cradling him in his arms like a baby.

Beron didn't object. Laying his head on the miner's broad chest, he appeared to go to sleep.

Willow and the prince exchanged glances. 'We'll follow you,' they said together.

Connor remembered. They were twins. He took a last look at the deeply shadowed cave, at the dying fire, and ran to where Thrak had disappeared into the darkness beyond the princess's renewed feeble light.

Relief at their escape and wonder at the discovery of his own magic filled Connor with a heady lightness. He might go home to his Forest after all.

Chapter Fifteen

Elder James' decision

'Where's Connor? Didn't you bring him home?' Lucy pushed past Gwen, rushing into the snowy lane, swinging about in search of her son.

For all Gwen had been dreading this moment, she hadn't come up with any words of comfort.

'No,' she said. Exhausted by her travels, Gwen longed to trudge the short distance to her home and collapse into her own bed. Sleep would be impossible however, until she told Connor's parents all of it. The villagers needed to be warned of a possible attack, too.

Gwen on Beauty, and Verian on her largest wolf, had journeyed swiftly through the Deep Forest. The rest of the wolf pack kept pace despite deep drifts which would have hindered people on foot – if they could have found the narrow, twisting paths wending between thick, raised roots which grabbed at unwelcome ankles and tripped unwanted visitors.

Verian left Maikin to defend the caverns, if needed. Gwen hoped it wouldn't be, for as far as she knew, Lady Melda was ignorant of the cavern-dwelling Danae.

Maikin pointed this out too, saying he and several guards should accompany Gwen. There was no need for Her Majesty to endanger herself. Verian's response had been gently firm.

'You and your guards cannot travel with any speed in this weather.' She exhaled heavily. 'Besides, my heart tells me wolves are needed in this battle, if battle there is to be. Not people.'

She would say no more, except the feeling was strong. Gwen worried what it meant, imagining what kind of army Melda might conjure with this Evil. Now Verian and her wolves had taken shelter in Peter's mill, waiting for Gwen's summons to the village.

Standing on the step of her sister's house, Gwen beckoned to Lucy. 'Come inside and I'll tell you everything.'

Lucy stopped searching the lane and chewed her lip. She made no move to go inside. 'Tell me now, please.'

'We've discovered where Connor is,' Gwen said from the step, 'and King Ieldon will do all he can to rescue the boys.'

'The boys, plural?' Peter brushed past Gwen into the lane. 'Come on,' he said to Lucy. He put an arm around her and helped her into the house.

Gwen went after them and shut the door on the icy night. No fire glowed in the parlour hearth, and the room was chilled. The only light was that which spilled from the kitchen beyond. There was warmth there at least, with the great cast iron range burning. A pot of stew bubbled, filling the air with a scent of savoury herbs. Unwashed plates filled a corner of the table, the sink was piled with pots, and the remains of a loaf of unwrapped bread lay beside its clay crock. Gwen frowned at the unusual mess.

'Where is our son?' Lucy demanded. 'Does that hateful woman have him?' She sat on the edge of a kitchen chair, staring at Gwen as if she would devour her.

Peter filled a kettle from the water barrel in the corner. 'Does she?' he said. 'Is it Melda?'

It didn't take long for Gwen to tell how she met Tristan in the Citadel, seeking help to find his son, Beron, whom Melda had definitely stolen. Also about the lady's attempt to kidnap the royal children, who had to be rescued by Asfal.

'Shame the gryphon wasn't here to rescue Connor,' Lucy said bitterly. 'The witch has them then.' She leaned forward, shoulders tense. 'Where?'

Peter poured boiling water into a large pot and set it on the table, bringing mugs from the sideboard to sit beside the pot. 'Yes, where?'

'We believe in the caverns of the High Alps of Asfarlon …'

Gwen told the story of the Evil from aeons ago and why the gryphon pendant Callie wore had been forged.

Lucy's face grew more pale as the tale went on. The undrunk tea grew cold.

'She wants revenge, on all of us,' Peter said, when the story was done. 'And if this Evil lies there still … if she wakes it …'

'Yes,' Gwen whispered.

Lucy's face was white. She reached across the table to grab Gwen's hand. 'Tell me I'll hold my son again, please tell me.'

Gwen covered Lucy's hand with her own. 'King Ieldon, Callie, Asfal – we must trust them to find a way. We can do nothing from here except make sure Connor has a home to return to when he can.'

Lucy rocked on her chair, her jaw clamped tightly as she tried not to cry. 'You're right,' she said. 'Wailing and moaning achieves nothing. My son needs me to have courage.' Her voice was strong, determined. 'What should we do?'

Peter stood up. 'We should tell Elder James immediately. Tonight. Melda could be on her way, bringing whatever wickedness she can conjure.' He rubbed his hand through his hair, his face strained.

'Will James believe us?' Lucy said. 'Or will he scoff at our wild imaginings, like he did before?'

'We can try.' Gwen gave a small smile. 'I've brought something quite persuasive with me, which might convince him we're serious.'

'No point going to his home. He'll be at the inn,' Peter said.

Gwen frowned. 'Do we dare confront him there? With half the village ready to follow whatever he says?'

Peter pulled at his chin. 'At least it'll be the villagers who decide to ignore us, not James alone.' He raised his eyebrows. 'Seems fairer, don't you think?'

'We have to warn everyone tonight, whatever they make of it. For Connor.' Lucy jumped up and fetched her cloak from the hooks by the door. 'I say we try it. What can we lose?'

***

Gwen pushed open the inn door into a fuggy warmth of pipe smoke filled with noisy chatter. No one paused to acknowledge her return. They were used to her occasional trips and added this habit to the sum of her general unnaturalness. Like the black horse she kept, and which she often rode into the Forest, returning with flushed cheeks and wind-blown hair even on the calmest days. A secret lover, hidden in the trees? Despite Gwen's strangeness, the villagers were happy enough to seek her out when in need of an ointment for a blister or a tonic for a child's cough.

Gwen searched for James and found him with other Elders at a table by the fire. She wriggled among the noisy crowd, approaching directly to ensure he saw her. He frowned briefly, and carried on talking.

'Elder James, can I have a word?'

James screwed up his eyes, his eyesight not what it used to be. 'Can't it wait?' he grumbled. 'I'm with friends.' He gestured at his companions.

'No, it can't.' Gwen raised her voice. 'I need to tell you and the Elders that the Sleih Seer, Lady Melda – the one who was in league with the Madach to sell the Danae into slavery – is holding Connor hostage.' She paused. A few eyes were on her. 'And we believe she's likely to attack our villages.'

James snorted. 'Why would she kidnap Connor?' he said, ignoring Gwen's warning. 'What value is the lad, except to his doting parents?' He sniggered his contempt. 'What could they give this lady in exchange for their son? Is she in need of a bag of flour?'

Other Elders tittered. Four villagers standing nearby stopped their chat to listen.

Gwen stifled her anger. 'She is in need of revenge.'

'Revenge?' James swatted away Gwen's statement. 'I have no memory of this Sleih Seer, and certainly none to warrant her wanting revenge.' He glowered at Gwen. 'You and your sister might believe in fairytales. Others have more sense.'

Keeping her voice loud, Gwen said, 'As well as Connor, she has taken another boy, the son of Tristan, Lord of Etting. You must recall Tristan, Elder James?'

'Of course I recall Sir Tristan. Lord of Etting, you say?' He put his fingertips together. 'I'm sorry to hear of his problems. However, Etting's an awfully long way from here, over the southern oceans. Impossible the two incidents should be connected.'

'Yet they are,' Gwen insisted. 'And while kidnapped children might not be of importance to you, the defence of the villages should be.'

'You're as bad as your poor mother used to be.' James sighed heavily, a pretence of compassion at their mother's passing a year ago. 'Your fey sister too.' He raised his eyes to the smoke-swathed ceiling. 'Always wanting the Danae to defend themselves from imaginary enemies.'

'Imaginary?' Lucy stood beside Gwen, her hands bunched into fists at her side. 'The Madach forcing everyone into one village, leaving our homes and gardens to rot?'

'Making us build a wall to create our own prison?' Gwen said.

'Neither of you were here, if I recall.' James scowled. 'You have no idea what happened.'

'I was here.' Peter joined them. 'I'm sure what happened.'

Around them, the inn had fallen into silence, some frowning at the exchange, others smirking at these old and new tales told by the strange sisters.

'I'm sure too, James.' The grave voice came from a corner table.

Matthew, the blacksmith. Thank the Beings. According to the tales Callie told, Matthew constantly begged for action right from the start of the Madach arriving under Captain Jarrow. He had never trusted them. He strode forward. The crowd parted for him. The smirks faded.

Into middle age, it was more than Matthew's rocklike girth and muscled arms which commanded respect. A man of few words, when he did speak, what he had to say was measured and thoughtful. Many, including Gwen, wished Matthew was their Senior Elder. He had shown no interest in the role, preferring to keep to himself and his forge since the death of his wife from a lingering illness several years ago.

'I was there,' Matthew said, eyes fixed steadily on James, 'from the beginning to the end, when we burned the gate in the fence the Madach forced us to build to imprison ourselves. I saw the miracle of the trees. I watched Callie and the young gryphon battle this Lady Melda for the necklace Gwen carried with her from the Citadel. And I saw Callie win.'

He stood back, arms crossed. A handful of the older villagers nodded, slowly, memories restored. There were mumblings. 'Yes, I remember too.' 'That Jarrow fellow, forever shouting, letting us out only to work our farms.' 'Where were the Elders during all this?' 'They locked away our Senior Elder, didn't they? Put him in prison on their ship when he stood up to them.'

James' heavy grey brows beetled. He waved his hand. 'You were always hasty, Matthew—'

'He's right, though,' a woman called.

'Yes. The lady was furious,' a man on the other side of the fire reminded the room. 'The Sleih king took her somewhere, do you remember?'

'And she wants revenge, on us?' an Elder said, shifting on the bench away from James.

'Yes,' Gwen said. 'On us and anyone else who was there. Which is why we need to defend ourselves.'

'Yes, yes,' voices called. 'She was a nasty piece of work.' 'She was.' 'We shouldn't take her lightly.' 'Best be prepared.'

James wasn't giving up. 'Assuming we need to defend ourselves,' he called above the rumblings, 'how do you suggest we do so?'

'Oh.' Gwen grinned, wolfishly (she hoped). 'I've brought help, like last time. It will be my pleasure to re-introduce you to them, Elder James.'

Chapter Sixteen

Escape

Willow couldn't sustain the light she had conjured much longer. It floated above her shoulder, barely bright enough to show Thrak striding ahead. Weakened by the struggle with the wraiths, her magic had had no time to recover. Her body craved rest, not a fast hike along rock-strewn tunnels pitted with holes. Thrak forged through the blackness, confident of his choices when paths diverged. He had mined these tunnels, and the centuries since those days hadn't dimmed his familiarity with their twisting turns.

'Will we ever get there?' Rowan whispered from behind Willow. 'Wherever *there* is.'

'I trust the miner.' Willow glanced at Connor, walking beside her, a grubby fur wrapped about him like a cloak. 'He's in your Aunt Callie's book.'

'Book?'

'Yes. An extremely ancient book with a long, hard-to-remember name. It tells how and why the gryphon pendant was made, to defeat this Evil which Melda's woken after all this time.'

'Thrak is from then?'

'And Olban. He let the Evil take hold of him. The wraith wasn't the real Olban. The Evil used his body.'

'Look!' Rowan pointed past his sister to a tiny white spot in the distance. 'It's daytime. We've been in here all night.'

Willow's weariness faded. Her legs wanted to run to the whiteness. Ahead of her, Thrak's footsteps quickened.

'Sunshine. I had forgotten the gleam of sunshine,' he

muttered, leading them to the opening.

Stumbling out onto the side of the mountain, Willow blinked at the sparkling brightness of dawn sun on snow. A weathered rectangle of rock overhung the entrance to the tunnel, rusted hooks driven into it where miners once hung their lanterns. There would be a track leading somewhere, of no use to them hidden under a white blanket. Willow shaded her eyes and squinted into the dazzling blue sky.

'Asfal will find us,' she said.

'Asfal?' Connor jerked his head to stare at her.

'Who's Asfal?' Thrak set Beron on a stone under the overhang, easing him down to rest on the sparsely grassed slope of the hill. The boy was awake, peering into nothing with frightened eyes.

'Yes,' Willow said to Connor, and to Thrak, 'A gryphon. He brought us here, and he's watching in case Melda returns.'

'Or Jarrow,' Connor said, twisting about to scan the skies in all directions.

'Who's Jarrow?' Rowan asked, at the same time Thrak said, 'Lord Gryphon sent a Hunter with you?'

'There is no Lord Gryphon, not anymore,' Willow said. 'Or Hunters. Or any other gryphons.'

'No gryphons?' Thrak's dark eyes grew sad.

'Asfal hinted there *might* be other gryphons,' Rowan said. 'Somewhere.'

'And Jarrow,' Connor interrupted, 'is a Madach captain who once tried to sell the Danae off as fairytale slaves. He's thrown in his lot with Melda.' He rubbed his head. 'A loud bully.'

'Don't let him hit me.' The distraught plea came from Beron, hunched on his rock, his arms shielding his face.

Willow ran to him, crouched, and touched him lightly on his shoulder. 'It's okay, Beron. He can't hurt you anymore.' She hoped it was true.

She lifted Beron's chin and gazed into his red-rimmed eyes. *Asfal, if you're nearby, please come quickly. This boy needs you.*

'Is that …? Is that … the gryphon?' Connor pointed to a large, winged shape falling out of the air towards them. His voice trembled, excitement and disbelief mingling.

Relief washed over Willow. They couldn't be out of reach of the tunnel too soon.

Asfal landed and folded his great wings.

Well done. He bobbed his eagle head at Connor and Beron, his eyes lingering for an instant on the leather collar.

'Aunt Callie's Asfal?' Connor's eyes were so huge Willow worried his eyeballs might fall out.

'Yes.' She touched the gryphon's golden flank. 'Beron's mind is sick. Not just Melda and her wickedness. There's a man, a Madach captain called Jarrow, with her, and he's mistreated the boys.' She pointed at Connor. 'Connor's fine, but Beron needs help beyond what I can give.'

Jarrow? Asfal said.

'You've crossed paths with him before?'

I have. The hint of lion growl suggested Asfal had unpleasant memories of the captain. *Let me help the boy.*

'One gryphon remains?' Thrak's forehead creased. 'And why doesn't he speak?'

Who is this?

Willow swung her head from Asfal to Thrak. 'Too many tales to tell, too much to catch up.' She softly squeezed Beron's shoulder. 'Please, Asfal, see what you can do for him. We have to get away from here.'

***

The voices of Beron's rescuers tumbled in his brain like waves washing over rocks, and as meaningless. Willow, Rowan. They were their names. He tried to grasp them, hold onto them, fighting the image in his head of cowering in the cave at the feet of a screaming Jarrow. He strained to listen to the soothing words of the dark-haired girl – Willow. Vaguely, he was aware of sunlight on his head, and of cold, fresh air not smelling of sweat, stinking animals, and cooking meat.

Now a new terror unfolded in front of his clouded sight.

A huge beast. At the front, it was a massive, blue-feathered eagle, with a terrifying beak, and – Beron dared to glance at the beast's feet – curling, cruel talons. Its back end was a lion with skin like pale amber. A long, tufted tail waved above its haunches. Beron struggled with a memory. There was an image of such a beast in his father's study, including the blue feathers. Once, when he stared at it, his father said it was a painting of a dear friend. Beron laughed, thinking it a joke, and Father smiled and said no more.

And here it was. The picture come to life. Bigger than he could ever have imagined. Beron stared open-mouthed. His whole body trembled and his throat jumped with nervous gulps.

'This is Asfal. He's a gryphon,' the girl, Willow, who had been nice to him, said.

Gryphon? Beron remembered the word from a moment ago. Someone had talked about gryphons, hadn't they?

'Asfal will take the fright away.'

Willow trusted the beast, and she wanted Beron to trust it too. Not it, him. Asfal. He would try, for Willow.

Beron clasped his freezing hands tightly together and forced himself to keep his eyes fixed on the gryphon. It was hard. He shifted his head from side to side, nervous, wondering how the frightening beast – Asfal – could take his terror away.

And yet, a calmness soon began to settle inside him, like a cape woven of delicate silk thrown gently over his fears to smooth the fiercest edges, make them bearable.

Beron felt the warmth of the sun as it rose higher, saw the snow sparkling. The boy, Rowan, fidgeted. Connor, like Beron, never took his eyes off the gryphon.

At last, Asfal ruffled his wings and looked at Willow. He bobbed his head, and it looked like he was speaking to her.

'I understand,' she said. 'The poor boy has suffered badly. He must be tough to have survived this far.'

'He'll recover?' Connor asked.

Beron wanted to tell Connor he thought he might recover. He stood up from the rock, his legs shaky, his head light, and faced the gryphon.

'Thank you–' he began.

'We've lingered too long.' The giant who had carried him from the cave interrupted. He crouched by the tunnel, listening. 'Creatures on four feet and two run this way. They are swift.'

Fear's rude and ugly head thrust into Beron's calm. He fought to push it down while the others rushed into action.

Willow pulled him from the rock, calling to her brother and Connor to help.

The giant strode over and lifted Willow, Beron, and finally Connor onto the gryphon's wide lion back in three rapid moves. Rowan vaulted on, last in the line, throwing his cloak over his shoulder to expose the sword he'd used in the cave, resting in its scabbard.

'Go!' the giant boomed.

Asfal lifted his wings, lowering them when Willow shouted, 'We can't leave Thrak behind. Wait.'

'The gryphon cannot carry us all.' The giant scowled at the tunnel, where a noise like low thunder reverberated from the opening. 'There is a place …' He took great strides through the snow and vanished behind a boulder.

White monsters poured from the tunnel, baying, growling.

'Watch out,' Connor shouted.

'Hang on,' Rowan cried.

Beron's heart bashed against his ribs. He wanted to be sick. Willow flung her arms around the gryphon's neck, and Beron tightened his grip around her waist. The magnificent beast rose into the air, lion claws and eagle talons scraping the heads of the surging creatures.

'Take that,' someone screamed.

Beron caught a flash of shining metal and the white creatures tumbling in a writhing heap. A cat-like monster with two heads and two sets of gnashing teeth leaped from the tangle. It launched itself at the gryphon.

A sickening crunch, a jolt. The gryphon faltered. Beron's stomach rampaged like a caged lion. He clung tighter as the world tilted.

Chapter Seventeen

A terrible message

All day and night, never resting, the monstrous army prowled the churned ground at the base of the Citadel's walls. Guards patrolled the battlements, on constant watch for reptilian creatures with outsized claws and bulbous eyes climbing the smooth stones. Spread thin along the length of the walls, Seers responded to cries alerting them to another attack, casting magic green fire to destroy the reptiles. None of the creatures had reached their goal. So far.

Callie walked the ramparts in a blustery, pale pink dawn, grateful Melda was unable – yet – to cast her spells on birds. She stopped, gazing northwards to the High Alps of Asfarlon, their peaks shrouded in snow-filled clouds. The knot of anxiety in her chest tightened further.

Princess Emeryn had discovered Willow and Rowan missing the day before. When they did not breakfast with her, she assumed they had slept late, still recovering from their ordeal with Melda. She finished her meal before checking. Both rooms were empty.

Callie had been to Asfal's stall, surprised to find him gone without telling her. Coming inside, she met with Emeryn on her way to the stables to search for the prince and princess.

'Have you seen the children?' Emeryn asked.

'No, and Asfal's gone,' Callie said, understanding in the instant what had happened. Worry for Willow and Rowan and anger at Asfal surged inside her.

'Their boots and warm cloaks are missing.' Emeryn's green eyes widened with alarm. 'You don't think …?'

'… Asfal has carried them to the High Alps …' A statement.

'They think to rescue those boys themselves?' Emeryn's panic bled into her soft voice. She put a slim hand to her chest, whirled about, and raced along the passageways to the king's study.

When questioned, the night watch said they spied the gryphon in the air around the Citadel. The sight surprised them because they'd been told he was injured. They were delighted he had recovered and kept guard with them in the dark night. He had flown low over the enemy's camp, setting up a howling and shrieking from the monsters which had driven their mistress from her pavilion. She shook her fist at the gryphon, and he flew high, disappearing into the starlit sky. Hadn't he returned to his luxurious stall?

A search of the Citadel brought no sign of the three, excepting the sword Celeste was missing, and prints showed that boots too small for adults had trailed through the kitchen gardens to a wall. No prints were found walking away from the wall. Neither were there eagle or lion prints to suggest this was where Asfal had flown from, carrying Willow and Rowan.

The king listened, stroked his beard, and called off the search.

'They have taken a secret way out,' he told Callie, who hadn't been aware of this secret way.

'We must send soldiers after them,' Emeryn demanded. She paced the king's study, gazing out the window where snow fell in great wet flakes, as if she would conjure her children to appear out of the sky by force of will.

'No.' King Ieldon's brow furrowed. 'I wish they had not done this, but Willow and Rowan have strengths to call on, and they are with Asfal.'

'It might work,' Callie said, frantically searching for ways to convince herself and the princess. 'Enough magic to stand against whoever or whatever guards the boys, yet not enough for the Evil to be too early prepared.'

'Work?' Emeryn snapped. 'Two children against this Evil which hides in those caverns? And who knows if those boys are even alive?'

'They're alive.' Callie tried not to let her own fears make her snappish too. 'Melda needs them.'

'And she is here,' the king said, 'weakening whatever guard she has on them in the caverns.'

'Exactly!' Emeryn pounced. 'Soldiers could bring them home.'

'No.' The king held up a hand. 'Consider, Emeryn. They'd have no idea where to start. Asfal, who knows the High Alps, and my grandchildren, your children, are Connor and Beron's best chance.'

Emeryn stared at her father-in-law. Her jaw quivered. 'You may be king, Ieldon, but I will hold you accountable if they do not return safely to me,' she said, and ran from the room.

The king and Callie had faced each other. 'It might just work,' Callie said again. 'It might.'

Callie stayed for a moment longer on the walkway, staring north, hoping for a reassuring whisper. Within the icy wind gusting over the battlements, a more frigid touch, like a frozen finger, probed her mind. She startled, stepped to the parapet.

Melda stood below, wrapped in a deep blue cloak dusted with snow. Her white hair glittered with sapphires and diamonds. Grunting, slavering bears with bulging lumps on their backs and curling claws surrounded her. They reared on their hind legs, lumpen paws lifted as if they would scoop Callie from the walkway. Melda held a tall bronze rod in one gloveless hand. A large diamond glinted at its tip.

'I see you, little witch.' Her shrill voice scaled the height of the wall like a ladder thrown up in a battle.

Guards either side of Callie notched arrows to their bows.

'No,' Callie told them. 'She's shielded herself in magic, it's dangerous—'

'Take that, evil one.' A young guard to Callie's left loosed his arrow.

Melda raised a hand, palm forward. A burst of blue and silver flames, and the arrow quivered short of its target.

Callie pivoted to the guard, a warning on her lips. The arrow swung around to its owner. The point pierced his chest.

He fell, screaming, to the stones. Acrid smoke rose from the wound.

'Take him to the healers,' Callie said.

Two guards lifted the wailing man and ran to the stairs. The remaining soldiers held their fire, wide-eyed, muttering about who was the witch and malicious magic.

Callie stepped closer to the parapet. The icy finger probed her mind. She threw up a defence. Too late.

'You tell me nothing new.' The victory in Melda's shrill tones chilled Callie's bones. 'I have a message for Ieldon.' The Seer snapped her fingers. Two bears, one each side of her, lifted their front paws in offering.

Callie's heart hammered, understanding a new horror was about to unfold, not wanting it to become truth.

The bears held two items. A leather flask, and – Callie drew in a breath, no – a long, rich blue feather. Melda touched the items with the diamond. They lifted from the bears' bristly paws to slowly float up the height of the wall. The rising sun burnished the blue of the feather and polished the brown flask to copper.

Callie's mouth went dry. She clutched the stones, scratching them with her nails.

'The gryphon is dead,' Melda called, with relish, 'torn apart by my beauties, my own creatures.'

Callie's gut melted to water. The guards on the wall stared at the items hovering just beyond their reach, teasing, tantalising.

'Thank you for sending me more pieces to bargain with.' Melda threw back her head, and when she spoke, ice sharpened her voice to a knife-edge. 'Tell Ieldon, it's the pendant or my new, sweet little friends will suffer the same as the gryphon.'

The vision swam, nauseating, before Callie's blurring eyes. She steeled herself, let her grief and anger carry her through the moment. 'You won't win this, Melda,' she called. 'Like last time, Gryphon magic will defeat you.'

'Stupid brat. Didn't I just say? No gryphon remains to stand by your side. You are abandoned.'

Along the wall, murmurs rose. 'The gryphon is dead?' 'Is

that where the prince and princess are?' 'What's this pendant she wants?'

Melda's laughter rang in the cold air. 'Yes, he is dead.' She waved the bronze rod. The flask and the feather edged nearer the wall. A soldier snatched them from the air. 'More creatures heed my call. It's a matter of time, little witch. Your soldiers will not hold against me for long.' With one last jeer, she strode away. The bears dropped to all fours to trail behind like a lumpy train.

The soldier who caught the feather and flask offered them to Callie. Foreboding and fear mingled in his eyes. Other guards who had seen the exchange looked to her, questioning.

'It can't be true,' she said. 'I would feel it, here.' She pushed her bunched fist into her chest, where grief and revulsion filled her lungs instead of air. 'If she had the prince and princess, if Asfal was … dead … she would have brought more than these … these … trinkets.' She reached for the feather, caressing its silky strength, and for the flask. A lump rose at the engraved 'Willow' on its side.

How she wished her assurances to be true. They had to be true.

She held herself straight, threw out the hand holding the feather to take in the massed white monsters beyond the walls. 'We are strong. We will defeat this evil.'

**

In King Ieldon's study, Callie sat on a high-backed chair and stared at the feather resting on a gold-embroidered velvet cushion.

The leather water flask which she had carried to him was not with the feather. Princess Emeryn had snatched the flask from the king's hand when told of Melda's message. Snatched, and hugged to her chest while she shouted at her father-in-law he was to blame, as she foretold, and he must send soldiers to rescue her children – his grandchildren, she reminded him.

The king listened with sad, sympathetic eyes. When Emeryn had shouted herself out and stood with chest heaving, her body taut with fury, he responded.

'I share your grief, Emeryn,' he said. 'Every instinct I hold as a grandfather screams at me to immediately assemble a small army and fly to the Alps to search for Willow and Rowan.'

'Yes.' Emeryn squeezed the flask more tightly.

'But you understand I cannot,' the king said. 'My kingdom with all its people, all its children, mothers, grandfathers – they are all in my care.'

Emeryn gasped. 'You refuse?' Her eyes were green slits in her golden face, her pretty mouth pinched in a straight line.

Ieldon held his arms out to her, an invitation to be comforted. She glared, not moving.

'Deep within you, Emeryn,' the king said, 'you understand the single assured way to bring home our children is to defeat Melda and her monsters.' When she continued to ignore his offered embrace, he reached out to touch the blue feather. 'I am in Council long hours, deciding how this is to be done.'

The princess had stalked from the king's presence in regal, sullen silence. Since then, she refused to leave her rooms. Meals taken to her were returned uneaten. She would see only Tara, her personal maid.

Now, staring at the feather, Callie's emotions cried out in agreement with Emeryn, although her head agreed with the king.

By the window, Ieldon stood with his hands clasped behind him, gazing into the night where a full moon glowed coldly among the ice-white stars. He had summoned Callie earlier, saying he needed to speak with her before he met once more with the Council, this time to tell his decision.

'It's my fault,' he said. His voice held a deeply sad weariness, and Callie's already full heart ached to burst in her chest. 'I should have sent after them as soon as I realised …'

'Sire, if Asfal is dead, every nerve in my body would tell me.' Callie spoke with a certainty she prayed wasn't simply wishful thinking. Besides, wouldn't Melda have brought more than a feather? Unless Asfal truly had been devoured. Bile rose up her throat. No, it was impossible. 'He must be injured,' she said, 'or there's another reason he hasn't been able to return.'

King Ieldon turned a drawn, weary face towards her, its shadows deepened by candlelight. 'I need your instincts to be true on this, Callie,' he said. 'What we do next depends on whether we believe Asfal is dead and the children captured.'

'The children are alive. Melda needs them and they pose no threat to her.' Unlike Asfal.

'Sire?' Emeryn's maid, Tara, curtseyed in the doorway. She held her skirt in trembling hands. 'I've a message from Her Highness.'

Callie strained to hear the maid's soft voice, as tremulous as her hands.

'Yes?' The king smiled a gentle encouragement.

'The princess says to tell you she's ready.' Tears pooled in the young woman's eyes. She brushed at them, hanging her head to hide them.

'Ready?' The king cast a puzzled glance at Callie, who frowned.

'Yes, Sire.' Tara spoke to the rug on the marble floor. 'She will exchange herself for the prince and princess as Melda's hostage. For the two boys also.'

'Ah.' Ieldon's eyes widened. He stroked his beard, where silver streaks had multiplied over the last few days. 'I see. Will you please ask the princess to come here so we can speak of this?'

Tara gulped loudly and continued to address the floor. 'She says, Sire, she will leave her room if she has your promise you agree to the exchange. Sire.'

Callie waited for the king's reply. He stared through the window, at the moon and stars, the blackness beyond. A log on the fire fell into the flames. Sparks hissed their way up the chimney.

Tara shifted from one foot to the other, daring to lift her head to peer at the king.

'Very well,' the king said. 'She has my promise.'

The maid dipped a hurried curtsy and swung about in the doorway. Her swift footsteps soon faded from Callie's hearing.

'Sire? May I ask what's in your mind?'

The king walked to a chair by the fire and fell heavily into it, his tiredness etched in every movement. He picked up a silver goblet of wine waiting on a side table, raised it to his lips, and sipped. Replacing it, he said, 'You may, although I'm surprised you need to.' He rubbed his chin. 'Do you suppose Melda would agree to such an exchange?'

'No.' Callie returned her gaze to the feather. 'If she did, she would have to produce the children. If she doesn't have them …'

For a moment, hope sparked, until the king said, 'If she does have them, she will not give up four valued and innocent young hostages for a princess not of our blood.'

'You will make the offer, Sire?'

'I will. For Emeryn's sake. She needs to do this. Let's see what comes of it.'

Chapter Eighteen

In search of fairytale slaves

'Go east? Hunting for Danae?' Isa's Uncle Viv shook his head, disgusted. 'You remember what happened last time?' He threw out pudgy hands greasy from the chicken bone he'd sucked on for his supper, his teeth not being what they used to be.

Isa's gaze wandered around the ramshackle robbers' camp settled among the leafless trees while she recalled that summer long ago. 'I remember you couldn't find these Danae,' she said, thanking the Beings for her father and uncle's failure.

She stoked the fire with a gnarled, charred stick. Golden sparks lit the frosty darkness. The camp had quieted for the night, people tucked up in their tents, wrapped in furs and dogs, except for Isa and a handful of others. These were the strongest of the men and women, those who hunted for food or raided the occasional farm or village for what they could find lying heedlessly about. Uncle Viv, well past his hunting days, was there as Isa's supposed counsellor, a role she rarely called upon since her more sensible da had passed several winters ago. Chester should have been there too, should have been their leader. Except he never recovered from his encounters with the Blue Lady. Hunched, his broad chest sunken, he spent his days outside his tent staring into the forest as if waiting for something, or someone, to appear.

'And the wolves,' Uncle Viv insisted, his two chins wobbling with emotion, 'what kept tracking us, blocking every path we could find.'

'The lady promised to send us a man who knows where these Danae villages are.' Isa withdrew the stick and laid it on the slushy ground. 'You were keen to find these fairytale people in those days. Now they're being offered to us, don't you think we should take the chance?'

'I was a kid then,' a tall, thick-muscled man said. He waggled a finger at Isa. 'I remember my da telling me how the lady don't like to be crossed–'

'–and why should we cross her?' The man's younger brother interrupted, all eager. He jiggled on his patch of log, his cloak slipping from one shoulder. 'We could do with a bit of luck, and some gold.'

A woman waved at the ragged tents around them. 'Be good to get new tents. These 'uns are getting beyond mending.'

'They are,' confirmed another woman. She lifted one foot from the ground, peered at the patched and re-patched sole of her boot. 'Shoes, too.'

'And new hunting gear, replace our blunt knives.'

Others took up the list of what the robbers needed.

'Do we agree we go with this captain?' Isa said. 'Find the Danae villages?'

Eager nods, except for one. Uncle Viv creaked to his feet, his belly wobbling above his short legs. 'I ain't going.' He waggled a finger at Isa. 'Don't care what your Blue Lady wants, it'll end in tears, same as last time.'

Someone hooted. 'Because you couldn't find 'em, don't mean to say we can't. 'Specially with a guide.'

'And how much does this guide get?' Uncle Viv demanded. 'How much'd be left for us?'

Isa gazed up at him. 'She said there's one Danae she particularly wants.' Lucy with the golden hair. Isa wasn't planning on allowing one strand of Lucy's silky hair to be given over to the Blue Lady. The robbers didn't need to know that, not yet. 'Once she's captured, it's up to us to agree the rest with the captain.'

'Humph.'

'There'll be plenty to go round,' Isa said.

The robbers babbled their enthusiasm for unforeseen riches.

Isa listened long enough to appear interested before saying goodnight and walking to her tent. Settled under her furs, she lay awake, staring into the blackness. She had won half the battle, which was how to find the Danae villages. The other half – how to turn things around when she needed the robbers on the side of the Danae – would be a lot trickier. She worried if she was doing the right thing. But how else could she be there to make sure Gwen and Lucy didn't become fairytale slaves after all?

She exhaled slowly and rolled over, hoping for sleep. Which came eventually, fleeing at dawn with a great yowling and barking of the camp's dogs.

Isa flung off the fur, shoved her feet into boots and grabbed her cloak before pushing aside the untied tent flaps.

'Oh!' She pulled up short, heart booming.

The dogs crouched against the patched tent walls, wailing their fear. The horses in their pen tossed their heads, whinnying and stamping their hooves. Those robbers who had ventured out to investigate, stood by their tent openings clutching bits of canvas, ready to bolt inside.

A thickset man with a cap pulled over greying ginger hair stood splay-legged by the deep red, ashy embers of the fire. His heavy, black coat came halfway to his knee-high boots. His leather-gloved hands held the reins of a young bay horse which foamed at the mouth. The horse's sides quivered with weariness, its head lifted, nostrils flaring and eyes showing the whites. Isa's heart went out to the exhausted, terrified animal.

The stranger, whom Isa assumed was the Blue Lady's captain, was not the source of the robbers', their dogs' and horses' panic. A pack of grotesquely deformed creatures, all white, some on four legs, some on two, milled about the captain. Slavering tongues lolled, filthy fangs bared, and red and yellow eyes gleamed in the low light. A rotting smell of meat left too long in the summer sun surrounded the pack like a miasma of disease. A low growl rose from their throats, cutting through the barking of the dogs like a snake sliding through grass.

Isa gathered her courage and stepped up to the smirking man. 'You're the captain the lady sent?' She had to raise her voice to be heard above the racket.

'I am. Jarrow's the name.' He peered steadily around. 'She was right,' he shouted. 'Bit of a scrapyard this place, hey?' He grinned a black-and-yellow-toothed grin. 'This might be your lucky day.'

Isa tilted her head at the monstrous pack. 'Your animals are frightening ours. Can you get them out of here while we ready ourselves to come with you?' She took another step forward, gesturing at the horse. 'I'll see to him. We've oats in the store, and water.'

Jarrow narrowed his black eyes. 'They won't attack unless I tell 'em to. They obey me.' He boasted his smugness like a boy whose puppy has finally bounded to him when ordered to come.

'Good.' Isa was abrupt. The monsters set her nerves quivering. 'Then command them out of here.'

The captain swept his hand over the pack and pointed to the edge of the camp, muttering in a low voice. Whatever he said worked, for the hideous creatures loped into the trees. Isa ignored them, grabbed the horse's reins from Jarrow and led it in the other direction, murmuring soothing sounds into its pricked ear.

She prayed to the Beings her promises to her people of all being well would hold. Her doubts at this uncomfortable alliance strengthened by the moment.

Chapter Nineteen

The bravery of Ilesse

Willow's world tipped. She clung to Asfal, her stomach churning. Beron gripped more tightly. If one of them fell, both would go. Behind them, Rowan screamed at the monstrous attackers.

A sickening crunch, a jolt which loosened her grip for a terrifying second, and Asfal tore himself free. He rose high, spreading his wings to carry them over the glittering sunlit valley.

Willow pressed her cheek into the blue feathers, her body tense, heart slamming. A gurgling sounded in her streaming hair. Beron. He whooped with joy, like a child being playfully whirled about in the strong arms of his father.

A tentative smile curled Willow's lips, until Asfal slowed, flew lower.

The cat thing, he said. *It tore my wing.*

Willow's smile fled. *We need to land?*

Yes.

One wing beat with its usual strength. The other struggled to lift high enough. They flew in a wide, jagged circle over a row of peaks to the next valley, gradually spiralling to land with a whumpf beside a frozen river which glistened in the late morning sun.

Asfal collapsed into the snow. Willow was off his back and inspecting the torn wing before the others had scrambled to the ground. A cluster of dark blue primary feathers were ripped away, exposing the chipped end of a long bone.

'Does it hurt?' she asked.

It throbs, which I could stand. And it will heal by itself, in time. But I cannot fly, not with all of you to carry.

Beron stood by Asfal's head. 'Poor gryphon.' His hand twitched towards the feathered head, stilled itself.

'Asfal can't fly,' Willow said.

'I thought so.' Beron peered at Willow. 'You can hear his thoughts?' When Willow nodded, the boy's eyes widened. 'Is it magic?'

'No.' Willow smiled. 'Simply the way it is. Sleih people can talk with him through his mind.' She stroked Asfal's neck and gestured to Beron to do the same. 'I'm extra lucky, because when he's close enough I can speak to him with my mind. I don't have to talk out loud.'

Beron took this in with frowning concentration, his hand laid gently on Asfal's feathers.

Connor joined the cluster, the tatty fur wrapped around him. 'If Asfal can't fly, we'll have to walk from here.'

Rowan, with Celeste still unsheathed, peered up at the craggy outlines of the alps. 'We will. Although to be honest, I don't like our chances of surviving the mountains in winter.' He bent to wipe the sword clean, and returned it to its scabbard. 'Besides, if we did make it, we'd run right into Melda's siege.'

There's help closer. Asfal nudged Beron with his beak. Beron squealed in delight. *The help we need to escape Melda's evil creatures.*

Again, Willow caught Asfal's swift glance at Connor's collar. Something about the collar worried him. More than the discomfort it caused its wearer, who constantly tugged at it, trying to relieve its tightness.

'Where's this help?' Connor asked.

Willow's eyebrows rose. Of course the Danae boy with his Sleih blood and Gryphon magic could hear Asfal.

Not so much where, as who. We have half a day until night falls. We must make the most of it. The gryphon heaved himself up, listing to the side. *Come on.*

The afternoon faded into a chilled, foggy dusk, like walking in a rain cloud. Willow's world constricted to Beron's bent back. The boy stumbled along in Asfal's uneven prints, dazed, his moment of joy riding the gryphon submerged by the slippery trek along a fog-shrouded valley.

Asfal wouldn't say where he led them.

We might not be welcome, he said, his eagle gaze concentrated on finding a way between the boulders and cracked ice of the stream. *I would not build hope where it might be dashed.*

'What happens if we aren't welcome?' Connor asked.

We will decide at the time. Perhaps my wing will be healed. Gryphons heal quickly.

'I think we're heading south and east,' Rowan said. 'If we keep going this way, we'll end up in the Deep Forest.'

Not so far, I trust.

Which was all the answer Asfal would give. Willow worried less about where he led them than about Beron. The boy's glee at being with Asfal had faded. During the short stops to rest, he refused to look at anyone, muttering curt answers when spoken to. This was Willow's first meeting with him, and it could simply be he was shy, withdrawn. Except his earlier happy shout didn't fit with shyness, nor his response to Asfal's nudge. Something apart from the sheer drudgery of their trek worried him.

Connor walked close behind Willow, his heavy breathing – hampered by the collar – misting on her hair, his arms wrapped in the fur which was all he had to keep warm. Last in line was Rowan, Celeste glinting in his hand in case they fell across Melda's deformed creatures. Willow was glad of the sword's hard shine in the damp gloom.

They trudged through the heavy snow, accompanied by the huffing of their own panting and the squeak of snow under their boots. Willow fretted about their need for shelter and a fire to survive the night. And food. The bread, cheese and handful of dried fruit which remained in her bag would not go far to fill their bellies. She was about to ask Asfal if he had a plan for stopping, when Rowan called out. Her pulse beat hard before she understood it wasn't a warning.

'Over there.'

Rowan pointed Celeste through the watery air. 'It might be

shelter.' He veered off their footprint trail, plunging into knee-deep snow.

Squinting, Willow could make out a deeper darkness on the shadowy slope of the valley, partially hidden by a tumble of rocks.

'Asfal,' Rowan called, more loudly. The gryphon halted, turning his head to listen. 'We need to stop before night falls, try to light a fire.' He waved at the darkness. 'It's a cave. Might be deep enough to hold us all.'

A dusting of snow covered the stony earth of the shallow cave, which would shelter the four of them if they squeezed together like kittens in a basket.

Well done, Rowan, Asfal said. He lifted his good wing to show the slim entrance to a gully running alongside the cave. *See if there's anything dry enough to burn. I heard running water further along the stream. Fish for our supper.*

'I should refill our water bottles.' Willow dropped her bag to the snow and opened it, thrusting her hand in to find the bottles. 'Only one? Oh, no.' She had given Connor the other when they were in the cave and had forgotten to collect it in their hurry to escape. She pinched her lips together. The lack of a container wasn't important, given they were hardly wandering in a desert. The flask was special, however. A gift from her father, engraved with her name. He gave it to her when she begged to travel with him. He had joked she should first practice her travels near the Citadel, and here was a flask to fill at every stream to remind her of her daddy, who loved her very much. She hated losing her father's gift.

Scowling, Willow re-tied the bag, keeping aside the remaining flask, and followed Asfal to where the water flowed.

***

In the last of the light, Connor, Beron and Rowan explored the gully, returning with armfuls of thin branches and dragging a short, thick log. Willow, returned from her water journey, stamped her boots, hugging herself from the cold damp which seeped into her cloak. 'Let's hope we can light a fire,' she muttered.

The wet wood took more of her weakened magic, helped by her tinder box, to set alight. When it was done, the four of them huddled together, holding fish skewered on sticks over the low flames. The dancing yellow warmth of the fire, the tangy, smoky smell of the wood, and the delicious aroma of baking fish, lulled Willow into feeling all would be fine, this first night anyhow. Especially with Asfal forming a barrier across the opening to protect them from whatever might lurk in the night.

'Is Asfal hungry?' They were Beron's first volunteered words since their landing by the stream hours ago.

'He ate his fish raw while you were getting wood,' Willow said. 'He's the least hungry of all of us.'

Beron's giggle sounded forced, jarring. Willow raised an eyebrow. She should have realised the boy needed time to recover from Jarrow's abuse and the sheer fright of his experience. Willow wished Grandfather was here to help him. He would make it right.

Connor pulled his fish from the fire and laid it on the flattish stone which served as a plate for them all. He ran a finger inside the collar, coughed. 'Is this a good time to tell what we think is going on?' He grinned. 'I thought I was clever because I'd learned from Aunt Gwen all about the Madach invading our Forest, and how the wild creatures fought alongside Aunt Callie to eventually send them packing.' He twisted to Beron. 'With the help of your father, who had to choose between what his father wanted and what was right.'

'He never talks about it,' Beron grumbled. 'If he had, I would've known who the lady was and run off.'

'I knew who she was,' Connor reassured him. 'Yet she stole me too. There's nothing you could have done.'

'Maybe.' Beron's voice wobbled. 'But when we were prisoners, you were the one who was brave. You didn't give in to her or Jarrow, or those creepy ghosts.' He stared into the fire, wiping a tear from his cheek with a vicious swipe. 'I'm a coward, weak. I can never be like my father, standing up for what's right.'

Willow glanced sideways at him. Here was what troubled him, was behind the morose silences. She lifted both her own and Beron's fish from the flames and placed them alongside Connor's.

'Not everyone is brave in the same way.' Willow put an arm around Beron's shoulders. He stiffened, but didn't pull away. 'Do you remember the wraith, Olban, calling to Ilesse when we were in the cave?' Willow recalled the kind spirit's guidance in the tunnels, the reassurance of her presence.

'I haven't a clue who she is,' Connor said. 'I thought he called you Ilesse. Then when Thrak said Rowan wasn't his prince, I realised this tale goes back much further than to our parents.'

'Prince?' Beron frowned at Rowan. 'You're a prince? And you?' he asked Willow. 'Are you a princess?'

Rowan laughed. 'I guess we didn't have a chance to be properly introduced. Yes, we're King Ieldon's, the king of the Sleih's, grandchildren.'

'How ...?' Beron sighed. 'Never mind. My tutor says I need to pay more attention to history and I think he's right.'

'You won't find this history in your tutor's books. These tales are much, much older.' Willow peeled off a piece of cooled fish and chewed it slowly. She swallowed, waved at the others to eat theirs. 'It's delicious. Thank you, Asfal.'

The gryphon blinked sleepily. *My pleasure.*

'So who is Ilesse?' Connor asked.

'Was Ilesse.' Willow took another bite of fish. 'A Sleih girl, about our age, training to be a Seer at the time the real Seer Olban was around.' She gazed past the fire to Asfal. 'It must have been a wonderful time, when the Gryphon and Sleih lived together in caverns in the High Alps of Asfarlon – where you and I went, Rowan, and saw the remains of their bookcases and firepits–'

'–and beds,' Rowan said.

Beron stopped chewing. 'Was she a coward too?'

Willow smiled. 'Just like you're not a coward, neither was she. She struggled a lot. The Evil touched her – like Melda and the cruel captain touched you – and wanted her to join with it, be its queen and rule the Sleih, the Gryphon, the Madach too.'

'She didn't give in?'

'Nearly, and here's what you need to remember, Beron.' Willow put her arm around his shoulder again and squeezed. 'She would've given in, except for others who helped her. A Madach girl called Gweyr, who turned out to be the Sleih heir – a story for another day. And a wonderful gryphon called Hestia who was the reason the Gryphon lost their ability to speak, because the Evil cursed her.'

'Is this all in the book you talked about?' Connor drank in every word, eyes shining.

'Yes. I haven't read it. Callie told me a few of the stories as part of my Seer training. She says it's to make sure we don't forget and can be better prepared for–'

'–what's happening,' Rowan finished. 'Celeste is in those stories too, although it's even older.'

'Do you see, Beron … Beron?' Willow smiled. 'He's asleep.'

Asfal opened one eye. 'As we all should be. Tomorrow will bring more hardship.'

Chapter Twenty

An offered trade

The cowards! Melda laughed out loud. Ieldon had sent his guards into hiding, ordered to their barracks, to protect them from her. Such a shame. To turn his own men against their king would have been a pleasure. Not until she learned what he had to say, however.

Above her on the battlement, Ieldon was flanked by the little witch — she who had stolen the pendant — and by a woman with the straight stance and steady gaze of a princess. Her long, black hair gleamed in the midday winter sun. Melda put a hand to her own once shiny dark hair, annoyed at the frisson of vain jealousy which ran through her. She turned her mind to more important matters.

Was Ieldon at last willing to give up the jewel, thinking he would save his precious brats? She smiled. Could it be this easy? Ieldon was ever weak-willed, listening to the counsel of those about him, seeking compromise. His willingness to appease might turn to her advantage.

At the base of the wall, surrounded by her favoured bears, Melda lifted her bronze rod with its gleaming diamond. She pointed it at the king.

'I am here at your summons, Ieldon, in the certainty you have come to your senses. Bring me the gryphon pendant, and the brats are returned to you.'

'I cannot do that, Melda.'

Her good humour fled. Anger roiled in her stomach. 'Then why am I here?'

'We are here to offer a trade. Princess Emeryn, beloved

wife of our son and heir, Elrane, and mother to our precious grandchildren, will go with you willingly in exchange for all four children.'

Elrane's wife. A worthy hostage. One to make the spoiled prince – absent, Melda assumed as his presence hadn't been sighted – squirm. If he was aware. Heartbreak would be harder if he had no knowledge of this deal. Tempting, nonetheless.

She raised the rod higher, pointed it at the princess. 'You offer yourself?'

The king frowned, likely expecting a straight refusal. They would see. First, she would have fun, restore her humour.

'I do.' The princess's arms hung at her sides, her gloved hands hidden in the folds of her fur cape. Her taut stance showed her desperation to see her children safe. Grief had scored lines on her pretty face. Melda probed the princess's defenceless mind, experiencing the pain, her longing for Melda's agreement. Melda drank it all in, storing it to pore over for later amusement.

She stretched the tension, feeling playful. 'You, a princess of the Sleih, would exchange yourself for the young royals?'

'As we have said.' Ieldon's voice carried across the milling hordes of Melda's beauties.

She planted her rod in the muddy slush. It quivered as if alive. Her bears crowded close, their stubby forelegs lifted in imitation of her own raised arms.

'Jump,' she called, grinning. 'We will catch you and take you to your children.' She waved her hand. 'A touching reunion.'

The king stepped closer to the rampart. 'An exchange is what we offer,' he said. 'You must return all four children, unharmed–'

Melda's grin widened as the grieving princess stepped to the wall, lifted her skirts and cloak and made to climb up. Ieldon grabbed her, pulled her from the edge. He wrapped his arms about her crying, struggling body. What a hero.

Melda soaked up the drama. Such fun.

'I will go to my babies,' the princess cried, like a baby herself. 'I will hold them in my arms. They can come home. I will stay.'

The little witch hissed at the princess. 'She has no intention of returning them, don't you see?' Her green glare bent to Melda, comprehending the game.

Of course Melda had no intention of giving up her hostages.Especially as she no longer had them. She gritted her teeth, squashing down the fury rising in her gorge as it had done on discovering her wraiths a pile of yellow bones, and her hostages escaped. Lucky the princess had left her calling card, in the form of the water flask. That, and the interfering gryphon's feather, were nearly as valuable as bargaining tools.

This game with the girl's mother appeased her, a little.

But now she tired of the drama.

'Stay, or come.' She took hold of the bronze rod. 'What worth is one princess, Ieldon, and not of your blood, when I have four beloved young ones in my care?' Melda grimaced. 'I've told you my price. The pendant.'

Her tones suddenly softened into a pleading cadence. 'A pretty jewel, so old as to be worthless, its poor magic surely faded completely. What harm to give it over?'

'Yes!' Emeryn ceased struggling, slipped from Ieldon's arms and knelt at his feet. Her voice fell clearly to Melda in the crisp air. 'Can't you see?' the princess cried. 'This is all for nought. That cursed necklace is merely an ancient talisman, carrying barely any power.' She raised her voice, pleading. 'As the lady says, what harm to give her the jewel? It's just a jewel.'

Melda continued probing the princess's mind, gentle, assuring. Above her on the wall, Ieldon stood straight and stiff, his face set, struggling with his thoughts as Melda turned her attention on him too. He stared out across the white siege. Melda waited.

***

The Seer's voice sounded as sweet to Callie's ears as honey on summer fruits tasted on her tongue. Her body relaxed, her mind became pleasantly hazy. Of course. The gryphon pendant's strength must have waned further since the time Callie and the Seer battled for its possession. As Emeryn begged, why not give it over? Willow, Rowan, Connor, and young Beron – their lives far outweighed anything Melda could do with the ancient jewel.

'No.' The king spoke at last. His voice, rusty and harsh, might have been dragged from the depths of the hidden caverns of Asfarlon. It carried a warning ... close your ears ...

Close your ears ... The haziness in Callie's head swirled, rifts opened. She became aware of Emeryn tugging at the king's cloak, begging, incomprehensible. What was Emeryn doing? Why ... the pendant, yes ... just a jewel ...

No. That wasn't right. Callie grappled with her sluggish brain. She wasn't thinking straight. No, no, no.

The king summoned Tara, the princess's maid, waiting out of view of Melda and her mind trickery. 'Take your mistress to her rooms.' He spoke in the same hard, uncaring tone, forcing out the words.

The maid came running, eyes wide at the sight of the princess's stricken distress. With unusual roughness, the king lifted Emeryn from her kneeling position and handed her, more gently, to Tara.

Callie barely took in the scene, straining to take control of her thoughts. Ieldon peered into her eyes. 'Callie.' He spoke with his normal strength, and an added urgency. 'Resist her.'

Resist? Yes, resist. One last effort and the murkiness cleared. Callie gasped. Swiftly, despite the sudden lethargy which made her want to sleep, she gathered her wits and threw up stronger shields against further mind-meddling by the Seer.

The king rested his hands on the parapet. 'Begone, Melda,' he called. 'Your tricks are to no avail here. We will not give in to your demands.'

Her joyless laughter rose to the battlement. 'Not even for the children?' Her voice hardened. 'I promise, Ieldon, you will live only long enough to regret this day. We swear it.'

She waved the brass rod and was gone in a blur of ashy, dark cloud.

The king breathed heavily. His golden face had paled to the colour of ripe wheat. Perspiration glowed on his skin despite the freezing air.

'We swear it?' Callie said softly, her own skin feverish, her heart pattering.

'The ancient Evil is near to taking her over completely.' The king straightened and looked out over the siege. His breathing slowed. 'To regain its fullest strength, the Evil needs more powerful magic than Melda has in her.'

'From the pendant.' Callie shivered as she wrestled with an idea. 'Sire, should we bring the pendant into the open, task the Seers with wakening its magic ourselves? If we can. Use it against Melda and this Evil?'

Ieldon pulled at his beard. 'If we can. I will think on it.' He watched the white monsters through narrowed eyes. 'It's a desperate measure, for if it falls into her hands already strengthened …'

Callie wrapped her cloak more tightly about her shaking body. Standing beside the king, she took in the vastness of the threat. She was heartsore at the loss of Asfal, and sickened by what Melda's young hostages must be suffering, imprisoned in the caverns below Asfarlon.

In the same caverns where once a young Sleih 'prentice Seer and a Madach girl who became a queen, together defeated this Evil. Callie frowned. And afterwards someone wrote the tale down as a warning, and to learn from.

The Ancient History of the Old Sleih, and How They Came by Their Magic through Ponderous Schemes and Long Collusions with the Fabled Gryphon of the High Alps of Asfarlon.

To learn from. Answers must be hidden in the vast tome, somewhere. Excitement rippled in Callie's veins as she ran from the wall, hurrying to her tower rooms.

***

Callie had abandoned the book to feed her rumbling stomach. She had begun at the beginning, and was working her way through its delicate pages, translating the Old Sleih, testing the ambiguities the language often threw up. Did a word mean this, or another thing altogether, and if it did, how did that change the whole meaning? The work was tiring, and her early excitement on the Citadel's walls had waned.

She sat at a small, cloth-covered table by the fire in her parlour, the remains of a frugal meal of cheese, bread, and soup before her. She ate slowly, savouring the taste.

Three days earlier, messengers from the King's Council had gone from house to house, asking for food to be rationed. Panic followed. Crowds descended on the marketplaces and street stalls, waving their coins, wanting to buy anything and everything they could. For the second time, Seers had gone among the people to calm anxious minds and restore order. Stallholders were asked to bring their stock to the Tower, where it was held for them in safety and daily amounts given out to be sold at normal prices. The Sleih and Madach within the walls had adjusted. Mostly. There would always be those who tried to profit from such a situation. Despite being hungry still, Callie set aside the cheese to save it for tomorrow. If they couldn't find a way to break the siege, hunger would soon be common.

Stirred by her anxiety, she pushed away from the table, ready to return to the book. She would study it all night if necessary.

Knocking at the door sent her into the hall. The evening was late, and her pulse fluttered at the idea of bad news.

'Callie, are you there? It's cold out here.'

The flutter turned to excitement. Mark had returned.

She pulled open the door and threw herself at her brother. 'Thank the Beings, you're here!'

'A warm welcome, thank you, sister.'

Callie dragged him inside, allowed him time to set his bag on the hall floor, and hugged him again. 'The prince, he's back too?' She led Mark into the parlour and to a chair by the fire.

'Yes. We were on the seas making our way here when the message came. An albatross had it from a seagull who had it from your owl, I think.' He grinned, his hazel eyes beneath his short copper hair glinting with good humour. 'Anyway, we made as fast time as we could.'

'The harbour? Has Melda taken it?'

'No, not yet. Somehow, Elrane received another message,

telling about the siege, so we sent scouts to see how things lay.' He pulled in his lips. 'That's a monstrous army the lady has gathered. But we were able to moor, unload the horses, and waited until night to fly here, singly, in the hope Melda won't realise the prince has returned.'

'Poor Elrane.' Callie poured a glass of dark ruby wine from a crystal decanter on the sideboard and handed it to Mark. 'What a dreadful home-coming, and today was awful. Emeryn is going mad, literally, with grief.'

'Emeryn?'

'Of course. You haven't heard it all.'

Callie sat opposite her brother, telling him what had happened since Melda had tried to kidnap Willow and Rowan, ending with the Seer's scornful rejection of the princess's offer to exchange herself for all four hostages. Mark's good humour slipped into a brooding darkness while he listened, the wine forgotten.

'Ieldon hasn't sent soldiers to find them?' he asked at the end of her tale.

'No. I agree with him. The king's first duty is to the Citadel and the people here. Besides, they would have no idea where to look.' She hunched forward. 'Deep in my heart I believe Asfal is with them, despite Melda's claims he's dead.'

'I hope you're right.' A frown shadowed Mark's forehead. 'And what about the Danae? Do you think she'll threaten them?'

'Doubtless. Gwen will warn them, and we have to hope Melda's too busy here to worry about a couple of remote Danae villages. For the time being, anyway. The same with Etting.'

Mark stood and paced from the fire to the window. He stared out, his hands clasped behind him. 'My whole being wants to go to the Danae, protect our people.' He swung around to Callie. 'The king is right, though. The battle, the war, will be won or lost here.'

Callie sat back in her chair, staring into the softly glowing embers of the fire. 'There's a way to defeat her. It's in the book. And I need to find it. Soon.'

Chapter Twenty One

Attacked

A bite of hard bread and cheese made an unsatisfactory breakfast, although Connor understood they must ration their scant food. The fire had sunk to grey ashes overnight, and he needed to shake off a light layer of ice from his tatty fur rug. His toes were so cold he could no longer feel them, his hands stiff and red. His neck ached and itched from the tight collar. For a moment, Connor imagined home. The iron range would be blazing. His mother would be shaping dough for loaves, and afterwards the tantalising scent of bread baking would set his mouth watering ... and beef simmering in a broth of herbs and onions ...

'Are you coming, Connor, or do you plan to stay here and freeze?' Rowan stowed Celeste in its scabbard.

Asfal waited beyond their shelter with Beron and Willow. The rising sun filled the valley with glittering light, etching their morning shadows sharply in the snow.

'Sorry, daydreaming as usual.' Connor shrugged the fur closer around him and stepped out of the cave. The sun on his head cheered him, however weak it might be.

They tramped beside the stream, no one talking. Connor stumbled through the calf-high fresh drifts. The collar itched badly, and he had to stop himself from reaching inside to scratch at it. His skin was raw, sore. He understood Rowan's reluctance to use the sword to get it off, only ... if it had worked ... No. If Rowan had tried, Connor might be a pile of ash like the cage. He gave the leather band another irritable tug and trudged on.

The sun was at its highest when Asfal stopped and peered up the slope.

We have to climb, he said. *It will be hard. We will need to rest on the way.* He studied the boulder-strewn hillside before beginning a zig-zag upwards trail.

Connor fell in behind the gryphon. 'I'm bigger than you or Beron,' he said to Willow. 'I can make the path wider, give you people prints to follow.'

Hand and footprints both. The four children floundered in the deep softness, the steep hill forcing them to use their hands in places to propel themselves forward. Asfal pushed with all the strength of his lion body, urging them on with *not far to go, see the ridge is in sight, we can rest there.* Something else, hints of a promise, lurked beneath his words. Whatever it was, Connor understood the gryphon was reluctant to say it out loud.

Gasping, knees aching, his skin stinging with the pricks of the tiny studs, Connor halted and glanced behind him. Beron had stopped too, taking deep gulps of icy air, peering down the slope. He jerked his head, bent forward to gesture to the valley floor.

'What's moving?' His voice squeaked with fear.

Willow followed Beron's finger. 'More than one, whatever it is,' she said. She grabbed Beron's hand and hauled herself and the boy up the hill, past Connor, past Asfal, who peered with his eagle eyes at the shadows between the rocks.

White creatures, he said. *Melda's monsters. As I feared.*

'They've seen us,' Rowan cried. He pulled out Celeste, the sword's edges glinting in the midday sun.

Connor stared at the creatures lumbering up the slope. Towards him. His breath caught in his throat as the collar tightened. Tall, with dull white fur, some with humpbacks, others with too many front legs, all with snarling fangs. There were too many for Connor to count. His body screamed at him to run after Willow and Beron, flee from this hideous death.

Courage, Connor. Courage, Rowan. Asfal's voice in his head, low, deep.

Courage. How had Connor done it before? In the cave with Willow. Delve for it, drag it up, from his stomach, through his heart and throat ...

'Come on, you monsters!' Rowan's scream jolted Connor's mind into action. He dug deep.

Beside him, Rowan brandished Celeste, readying to attack. Connor felt Willow's presence too, bending her energies on the creatures, as focused as Rowan's sword. Connor ignored the collar, drew in ragged breaths, desperately searching for his spark of magic.

On his other side, Asfal planted his eagle talons in the snow, lifted his head and opened his beak. Nothing Connor had heard compared with the sound which issued – high, piercing, like it would slice mountains, shatter stone.

The monsters faltered. For one moment, Connor's heart leapt. Victory was not theirs so easily. Another sound carried in the glittering sunlit air, low, ominous, dark. The white creatures lifted their ill-shaped heads. They gathered into a tight bunch and leaped forward, scattering snow, yowling, baying.

Rowan screamed, waving the sword. The creatures came on.

Connor would die here, on this freezing slope, his heart chewed from his chest by monsters ...

'No!' Willow's shout stabbed at Connor's brain. 'No, Beron!'

'Go away, go away!' Beron had run back. He bounced beside Connor, awkward in the snow, waving his arms at the deadly monsters, screaming.

The boy's courage galvanised Connor. Death would not find them here, not like this. Beron mustn't die. He reached out his mind to Willow.

Together, they fought to throw up a wall before them. A buzzing energy flowed from Connor's chest. He flung out his arms, expecting bolts of lightning to shoot from his fingers. No bolts, but a shimmering haze building ahead of him, like a shield. An opaque glass wall which rippled like the ocean below the cliffs at home.

The first white creature plunged into the wavering wall.

Connor jerked as it crashed through, like a rock thrown into a pond. Rowan plunged forward, flashing Celeste. The monster's head dropped to the snow. Its body followed. Both head and body disappeared in a black, smoky puff. An oily smell hung in the air.

Connor relaxed his guard slightly, until another — a cat-like animal with two heads, red eyes, fangs dripping black drool — crashed through the wall. Celeste flashed. Another head rolled.

The creatures didn't hesitate, driven by an unseen, terrible force. Three, four, succumbed to the sword. The wall weakened with each attack, gashes appearing in its wavering folds. Connor wheezed heavily, the collar ever tightening. His legs were reeds, trembling in the snow. He couldn't keep this up. Willow and Rowan needed him. Beron, jumping up and down beside him, yelling like a madman, needed him. He would fail. Desperation clawed at his chest.

Where was Asfal? Why wasn't he lending his Gryphon magic to theirs? How long before the monsters demolished their flimsy defence?

'Look up,' Willow shouted. Her voice cracked with exhaustion and terror.

Connor threw back his head to meet this new threat.

The wall collapsed like water flowing from a spilled bucket. The monsters reared, snarling. Claws and teeth filled Connor's view. He crossed his arms in front of his face, palms out in a futile attempt to save himself.

Willow screamed. Beron echoed her cry.

Chapter Twenty Two

Iron

The great book lay open on Callie's desk under the tower window, the bulk of its pages read. She carefully flipped over another fragile leaf, running her finger along the lines of faded script. The ancient Old Sleih lettering was hard to decipher. Her head and shoulders ached from hours of concentrated reading, and with disappointment. It would help if she knew what she sought.

The Citadel had become a stone-walled island rising from an ocean of dirty white fur, too-long claws and slavering jaws created by Melda and the Evil she had allied herself with. The return of the prince had momentarily cheered the besieged population, until it became clear there would be no instant victory. Everyone was hungry, with all food rationed, purchased by the royal treasury and given out daily according to need. Water, fortunately, still flowed from the numerous fountains set in the hillside.

Meanwhile, Callie pored over the book. Nothing had leapt out as a means to defeat this Evil and its creatures, except for the forging of the gryphon pendant. And how the pendant had been used wasn't clear.

She tugged gently on the silver gryphon with its blue sapphire-streaked wings and green emerald eyes which hung once more on its chain around her neck. King Ieldon had agreed to remove the jewel from the Citadel's vaults. Sleih Seers experienced in the most powerful strengthening magics cast their spells over the pendant to strengthen its magic as best they could. Whether it worked, no one could tell. Callie liked to believe the tiny gryphon, reclining on its side, beak closed, was warmer on her throat. She ignored the notion this might simply be her contentment at wearing it again.

Callie leaned back in her chair, stretching the stiffness from her shoulders. The fire had fallen into dull scarlet coals, and the chill touched her skin. Standing, she bent to the cast iron fire tools. Lifting the poker, she prodded at the charred wood to release the flames. As they sparked, the ghost of a memory stirred into life. Callie withdrew the poker, held it sideways and weighed it in her hands.

Iron.

She recalled the first day of the siege, when the soldiers fought the monsters while the refugees escaped into the Citadel. The loathsome creatures had died easily at the touch of the swords. The watchers had cheered the skill of the swordsmen. Was it only their skill?

Abandoning the poker to the hearth, Callie stooped over the book and flipped to the end. Additional notes had been made here in a different hand, less refined than the main recorder. They were written in the common tongue of the Madach and Sleih, making them easier for her to read and the meaning clear. The author was succinct, summarising a struggle between the Evil's malformed creatures and a group of wizards near a small village called Atias. Many believed Atias had become Ilatias, that the Citadel was built at the place this struggle occurred.

Callie had no interest in geography at this point. What she sought was – she whooshed out a yelp of triumph. There, plainly written:

'We discovered the loathsome creatures were terrified of our pikes and could be vanquished by contact with them. We assumed it must be the iron, but had no chance to test this, the magicians in Asfarlon completing their task and destroying the Evil to save us the need.'

'Iron,' Callie whispered to the black night outside her window. 'It's worth a try.'

***

'You believe our soldiers had an effect on the monstrous horde because they have iron swords? You think it's the iron which kills them, however it's wielded?' King Ieldon stood with his palms flat on his burnished desk. 'What about the arrow the young soldier loosed on Melda?'

Callie, seated on a tapestried stool by the low-burning fire, bit her lip. 'I thought about that, Sire. Maybe it's because the Evil hasn't taken her over fully yet. Her own magic was enough.'

'Which means she herself is immune to iron.' The king moved from the desk to pace in front of the fire. 'Will it work?' He rubbed his temples. 'Who will test this? And even if the book is right, how many monsters could our soldiers destroy before being killed themselves?' His strained face exposed his hopelessness.

'Sire.' Callie hesitated. 'With our own Sleih and Madach, plus the refugees filling the Citadel, we overflow with bodies capable of fighting.' Her words tumbled out in a rush.

'Send untrained Sleih and Madach to be slain by this dreadful enemy?'

'If they see the iron in action,' Callie said, 'they might be willing.'

The king peered at her, his deep green eyes troubled. He gave a sharp nod, as if a decision had been made. 'It's a chance we must take,' he said. 'None of us will have a choice if we don't find a way to defeat Melda.'

'Yes.' Callie understood she was not alone being woken in the darkest hours of the night by terrible visions.

King Ieldon walked to the door to summon the servant waiting in the hall. 'We will order iron to be collected from wherever we can within the Citadel and cast it into weapons.' He gave Callie a half-smile. 'We need a purpose. Activity will help us all.'

'Sire.' The servant met the king at the door. 'There's a messenger at the walls urgently seeking audience with you.'

'Messenger?' The king stiffened. 'From Melda?'

Callie grew cold. What new horror did the woman bring to darken their sleep?

'No, Sire. An eagle who has, I am told, flown here from the High Alps.'

Excitement mingled with Callie's dread. 'The High Alps? Does the eagle have news of Connor and Willow? Of Asfal?'

King Ieldon was already through the door. Callie rushed after him.

***

Patrolling guards with upright spears peered over the walls at the snarling creatures below, watching for any white-skinned reptiles attempting to scale the stones. Seers with their cloaks hooded warmed themselves at low-burning braziers scattered far apart along the walkway. The braziers' weak fires reminded Callie that wood, as well as food, was scarce in the Citadel.

The eagle's yellow claws clasped the surface of a merlon, the high stone of the battlement. With her striped brown-and-white wings folded tightly to her body, she had lowered her head in rest. The Seer who had been summoned by the guards to communicate with the eagle hurried forward at the king's approach.

'She has flown in great haste throughout the day and night and will speak only to you, Sire. She says she has a message of great importance.'

'Greetings, Eagle.' The king inclined his head. 'I am Ieldon, King of the Sleih. Will you tell me what you have learned in the High Alps of Asfarlon?'

The eagle raised her head. She peered at Callie. *Well met, Callie of the Danae,* she said. *We fought together when I was barely more than a chick, to oust the destroyer, Jarrow, from our Forest.*

'Well met, indeed.' Callie smiled. 'Were you with Child, I mean Asfal, when he led the eagles to attack Jarrow's ships?'

I was, and proud to fly with the young gryphon. She twisted her head to the king. *I recall you being there also, Ieldon. A worthy ally.*

'Thank you.' The king bent his head. 'That battle was won, and as you see, we face an old enemy again.'

The eagle fluffed out her wings. *This morning in the Alps I came across a Sleih, a giant of a man, making his way south. He hailed*

130

me, seeking my guidance on what lay ahead and how far he must travel to find the King of the Sleih, if such existed.

Callie crinkled her brow. If such existed? Where had this giant been all his life? 'Who is this Sleih?' she asked.

His name is Thrak, and he has been imprisoned in the deep caverns below Asfarlon. He had no idea for how long. He, and others with him, were woken recently by a powerful Seer, of the name Melda.

'Thrak?' Callie squeaked. 'Thrak is in the book,' she said. 'Melda must have woken him, and the Seers whom Olban transformed into wraiths, when she woke the Evil.'

'My grandchildren and the gryphon, Asfal?' the king asked the eagle. 'Does this Thrak have any news of them?'

The eagle lifted her tired wings. *He did not say, Sire. His mind grapples with his new freedom. He seeks answers to his own questions, not to answer others.* She blinked. *On learning a king still ruled the Sleih, he begged me to take a message.*

'And the message?' Impatience edged King Ieldon's tone.
The one who bears Celeste freed him.

Callie's heart skipped. She glanced at the king. Rowan, at least, was alive, and free. Or had been.

'Thank you, my friend.' The king bowed his head to the eagle before summoning a guard. 'At first light, we need two horses, one with no rider. They will accompany this eagle to the High Alps and return to us with a stranger. A Sleih by the name of Thrak.'

'He won't have seen a flying horse, Sire,' Callie reminded the king.

Ieldon gave his half-smile. 'There is much this ancient being hasn't seen. We will need to be considerate.'

***

Thrak's wonder at his flying mount and his awe at the Citadel's yellow-stoned grace failed to match his sorrow at the absence of gryphons from this new world. His shock at the dreadful siege overcame both.

Callie had met the riders at the tunnel – this way into the Citadel chosen to avoid Melda realising the one time wraith had been made whole again, should she not already be aware. Greeting Thrak, Callie told him she knew who he was and promised him a brief history in due course.

While Princess Emeryn paced a smooth furrow in her father-in-law's rich carpets, Thrak bathed and ate. Clean and fed, he sat with the king, the princess, and Callie to tell what he had witnessed in Melda's cave.

Emeryn's glowing pride at her children's bravery brought colour at last to her pale gold cheeks. Callie raised her eyebrows at Connor's role. Magic in the lad? Gryphon magic would help him survive, especially if he and Willow worked together, and with the sword … A sliver of the burden of the fear she carried fell away.

What Thrak told next, however, subdued her relief.

'Melda has a helpmate,' Thrak said. 'A sorry mess of a man.' He shrugged. 'For whatever reason, she appears to value him.'

'A helpmate?' Callie said.

'His name is Jarrow, a captain of some sort.'

Callie started. 'Jarrow has returned too?' she whispered.

King Ieldon briefly closed his eyes. 'Of course. He was there when Elrane and I … did what was needed. We let the captain go free.' He grimaced and softly slapped his palms to his desk. 'I should have seen they might join forces in their search for revenge.'

Jarrow? With Melda? 'No.' Callie's mouth went dry. 'Jarrow will want the Danae. He won't have given up. Which is why we haven't seen him here because …' She grasped the arms of her chair to steady herself. Gwen would warn the villagers, prepare them for an attack. They wouldn't be caught unaware. Although what could they do? Was Jarrow able to command the loathsome creatures? Had Melda given him that power? Her full burden of fear returned, a rock in her stomach.

'I see this man is known to you,' Thrak said. 'Jarrow wasn't there when we escaped. The spirits warded the way out, until they were destroyed.'

'Where are my children?' Princess Emeryn's tentative smile waited to be fully released with the knowledge Willow and Rowan were safe.

'We escaped the tunnels and met with the gryphon.' Thrak frowned, his gaze on the king. 'The creatures of evil pursued us, and we were set upon. The gryphon could not carry the children and myself to safety, so I fled to find sanctuary elsewhere.' He paused. 'I am sorry, Highness. I cannot tell you more.'

A low moan escaped the princess's lips. Callie shared her distress. All four could be Melda's prisoners, as she claimed. Asfal? She searched her heart. Sorrow, yes. Deep, heart-sickening grief? No.

She reached across to touch Emeryn's hands, clasped tightly in her lap. 'They are alive, Highness.' She tapped her fingers to her own chest. 'I feel it here.'

Afterwards, Callie sat with Thrak to tell him what they knew of the last days of Asfarlon. When she showed him the gryphon pendant he murmured wistfully, 'The work of Bakran and Mayar,' and a shiver ran up Callie's spine that this man had lived alongside those long dead Sleih who created the tiny gryphon. He did not know how it had been used to defeat the Evil. 'Olban imprisoned me early,' he said, with a touch of bitterness.

Now Callie had brought Thrak to the battlements to see for himself the extent of the siege.

'The Citadel cannot hold out forever.' She pointed along the walls to where Seers stood beside guards, watching, ready to act. 'The Seers with magic to destroy are few, and they grow tired, their magic needing to be replenished more and more often.'

Thrak laid his huge hands on the wall, scowling at the dirty, roiling mass which stretched far into the distance. 'You tell me it was thus at Asfarlon, these beasts clawing at our gate?' He frowned at Callie. 'The time I have learned were the last days, before the fire took my home.'

His deep green gaze turned inward, and Callie understood he grieved at the destruction caused by the ancient, other monstrous army. The one created by the same Evil.

'Iron,' she said. 'The book I told you about says iron might have been used to destroy the monsters. At a place called Atias, where there was a battle.'

Thrak frowned. 'Then why do you not attack with iron? Are the guards' weapons not iron?'

'Yes, but there are too few guards, not enough weapons. The king has ordered iron to be given up by households to cast into more weapons.' She waved her hand over the yowling monsters. 'As you can see, it's unlikely to be enough. Even if it works.'

'Not enough iron?' The boom of Thrak's laughter startled the guards nearby. 'The tunnel they brought me by is full of iron.'

Callie's eyes widened.

'Give me strong men and tools –' Thrak thumped the stone with his giant fist' – and I will give you iron to make weapons for every willing fighter in Ilatias.'

Chapter Twenty Three

Gryphon friend

Calm, calm. Asfal called, reassuring.

Connor swung about, seeking the gryphon, straining for rescue.

Asfal streaked out of the pale blue sky, talons extended, blue wings spread. He plummeted into the midst of the monsters. Baying and yowling, the loathsome creatures twisted away, clawing at their attacker.

Connor's heartbeat didn't slow. Two more gryphons – one black-feathered, one golden – fell on the creatures. Their beaks gouged the dull white fur. Their claws ripped the misshapen backs, and with each gouge, each bite, the monsters evaporated, vanished.

Connor blinked. If it wasn't for the blackened, stinking, trampled snow, the monsters might never have been there with their slobbering jaws and wild, red eyes.

He collapsed onto a rock, gulping air. His heart boomed. Rowan stood splay-legged where the magical, flimsy wall had been, Celeste forgotten in his hand. He stared into the sky at the three gryphons. Willow stumbled to Beron's side. The boy leaned heavily into her, white-faced, sweating. Willow's arm around his waist, her chest heaving, the two of them also peered into the sunlight.

The gryphons landed. Asfal, with his torn wing, staggered before regaining his balance. His lion legs trembled. The two strangers waited behind him, giant wings black and golden against their tawny bodies. Their tufted tails lay across the snow, twitching.

Sleih and Madach, I see. The golden gryphon's thoughts came strongly to Connor, like it was used to commanding others.

And a stranger. Yet he hears us. The black gryphon sounded hardly less commanding than its fellow.

Both gryphons swivelled their huge eagle heads sideways to fix Connor with dark eyes. He swallowed. They were with Asfal. They wouldn't hurt him. Would they?

'Thank you for saving us.' Connor could think of nothing else to say.

'There are more gryphons!' Rowan cried. He grinned widely. 'Why didn't you tell us, Asfal?'

Willow grinned too. 'You're leading us to Lord Gryphon? He reigns still?'

Asfal bent his head, his third eyelid closing and opening.

He wears a collar, the black gryphon said, lifting a long-taloned claw to point at Connor.

We smelled the magic before you summoned us, Asfal. A lion growl rumbled from the golden gryphon's eagle beak. *Bad magic. Why do you allow a traitor to accompany you?*

Traitor? Connor pulled at the leather band which marked him as an enemy. His skin itched.

'I'm no traitor,' he protested, his voice croaky.

He tells truthfully. The boy is honest. Asfal limped to stand between Connor and the gryphons. *The collar was forced on him. We need strong Gryphon magic to remove it.*

The black gryphon humphed. *So you bring him to us.*

Connor squirmed. These beasts weren't happy. Mainly about his collar. Connor wasn't happy about the choking band either.

Connor. Asfal's voice sounded tired and strained with the effort of speaking. *It is as I suspect. The collar allows Melda's creatures to track you.* He tilted his head at the strangers. *We will go where it can be removed.*

Beron leaned away from Willow. 'Are they friendly?' His wide eyes were ready to be frightened.

Tell Beron one needs to earn the friendship of gryphons, Asfal said. *They value honesty and justice, which is what you all must show. Bravery too.*

'I'm already honest. I believe in justice,' Beron insisted when Willow passed the message to him. He squared his shoulders. 'I can try to be brave too. I promise.'

'Please,' Connor said. 'A wicked man put this collar on me, like I was a dog. Please take it off.'

The golden gryphon shook out its wings and bobbed its head. *The boy needs us, Nessus. Can you not sense the magic in him? Did you not see how he fought?*

The black gryphon, Nessus, fluffed his neck feathers. *My apologies, Theia. I should have known* – he gazed at Rowan, or rather, at Celeste – *given the company he keeps. Nevertheless, I counsel caution.*

Asfal growled softly. Willow, eyes crinkling with concentration, gazed at the two gryphons. They peered back with a fierce intensity. Connor could make out nothing of what passed between them but was grateful when their rigid stance relaxed. When the mutual scrutiny was over, Willow rubbed her eyes as if coming out of sleep.

'I've told them who we are and why we're here, as best I can,' she said. 'They'll take us to Lord Gryphon.' She gave Beron an apologetic smile. 'Including the Madach.' She shifted her smile to Connor. 'And the one with the collar, whose lineage is hidden to them. I've explained, sort of.'

These gryphon hadn't heard of the Danae? How long had they been hidden in the mountains? Willow tapped Beron's arm.

'You're allowed to ride the golden one, whose name is Theia,' she said. 'She's agreed to carry you and me.' She swung around to Rowan. 'You and Connor can ride Nessus. He wants to keep an eye on the one bearing the collar, and he also wants to talk about Celeste. He can't believe you actually hold the ancient sword in your hand.'

The vision of home swam in Connor's tired mind. This time, he wasn't as keen to be there. Not when he had the chance to ride this warlike gryphon – whatever the gryphon's views on his honesty and lineage – to meet their lord and visit their halls. And get rid of the hateful collar. The oak tree and the teasing of his friends existed in a whole different world.

***

Asfal flew slowly and awkwardly behind Theia and Nessus, who circled occasionally to allow him to catch up. Willow watched, chewing her lip. The attack on the monsters hadn't helped Asfal's injury.

Their flight above the sunlit white alps was nevertheless short. They flew south and east, their backs to the winter sun as it lowered itself to the craggy, rose-hued horizon.

We arrive soon at the home of the Gryphon. They await us, Theia said. She swooped to a towering cliff rising from a slope above a frozen lake.

Willow imagined the scene in summer, the gentle slope bright with grasses and wildflowers, humming with birds and insects, while gryphons took their leisure along the shores of the glacier-green lake. In the late afternoon winter light, the unblemished snow glowed pink. Large openings, many fronted by stony ledges, pocked the burnished gold cliff face with violet shadows.

Theia made for one of the largest gaps, high up. Beron wrapped his arms tightly around Willow as the gryphon dove into the black maw. She landed in a massive stone-floored dim cavern smelling faintly of wet fur and blood. The home of the Hunters, Willow decided. Nessus followed close behind.

Last came Asfal, wings flapping awkwardly, his strength giving out. He fell to his side, beak open, panting hoarsely.

Willow squatted beside him, stroking his feathers, which had dulled to an unhealthy pale blue. She fought her panic and peered at Theia. 'Do you have healers? Will they cure him*?'*

We have already sought the healers, and they are on their way. Theia gently nudged Asfal's head with her beak. *The strain has been too much. He needs rest and care.*

'Can they help him?' Beron hovered nearby, one hand stretched to the gryphon, pain in his eyes. 'Will Asfal be all right?'

'Yes,' Willow said, praying it would be true. 'The healers are on their way.'

Theia bowed her eagle head. *Meanwhile, Nessus and I must*

take you to Lord Gryphon. He awaits us.

'I can't leave Asfal by himself—'

A busy rustling of feathers and a fast tap tap of talons and claws cut off Willow's protest.

Three grey-feathered gryphons hurried into the cave. One dragged a small, wheeled wooden cart bearing stone and clay jars, and translucent phials filled with colourful liquids which shone in the gloom. Another had furs heaped across their lion body.

The first gryphon bent the tip of her wing to her beak, her eyes blinking rapidly. *Our traveller returns, and in such a state.* She pinned Willow with an eagle eye. *Are you Callie? What have the two of you been doing?*

Willow's face grew hot despite the numbing coldness of the cavern. 'No, umm ... Madam Gryphon. I'm Willow.'

'She's a princess of the Sleih.' Connor stepped forward with a small bow of respect to the gryphon. He pointed at Rowan. 'And he's Rowan, her brother, the prince. He wears Celeste.'

Celeste? The gryphon healer bobbed her head. *I'm sure he does.* She bent over Asfal. His eyes were closed, his sides heaved. *And now you will all leave us to deal with our patient.* She waved her wing. *Furs please, let's make him comfortable given we mustn't move him yet.*

Come, Nessus said with a touch of impatience. *Asfal is in the best care, and we're keeping Lord Gryphon waiting.* He strode to the opening to the inner passageways, expecting them to follow.

'We'll let the healers take care of Asfal, Beron.' Willow took the boy's cold hand. 'We're going to see their Lord.'

***

Beron's grip on Willow's hand tightened and didn't loosen as they walked wide passageways of smoothed rock, and down many sets of worn, stone stairs. His gaze darted from side to side, taking in the richness of these halls high in the mountain, far richer than his father's castle. Late afternoon wintry sunlight spilled into the west-facing openings to suffuse the air in those caverns with dancing, glittering light. Rows of tall shelves were cut into the rock walls to display gem-studded ornaments and heavy, worn leather books. Fire danced in shallow pits dug into the floors, the warmth seeping through open doorways into the passages. Heavy furs carpeted the floors, and meadow hay was piled thickly on wooden frames.

'They have beds like the burnt one Rowan and I saw in Asfarlon,' Willow murmured, pointing into one of the caves.

The caverns on the other side caught no natural light, warmed instead by a yellow glow from sconces in the walls.

They continued, following Nessus. In one cavern, Beron saw a gryphon perched on his haunches, wings folded, front eagle talons turning the pages of a huge book laid on a stone workbench.

Several gryphon passed them in the hallways, and it didn't take any special magic for Beron to sense their suspicion of these two-legged strangers.

'They're curious about us,' Willow murmured after nodding politely to a tall, green-feathered gryphon.

'They don't trust us though, do they?' Beron said.

Connor felt it too. He fell back from walking beside Rowan. 'I don't think we're welcome here,' he said. 'Especially me.'

Willow pressed her lips together. 'Let's hope Lord Gryphon is more sympathetic and will help us go home.'

Whose home? A surge of longing for his parents, his pony, even his tutor, rose in Beron. Would Lord Gryphon help him too? He suspected Etting was a long way from these alps. Tears welled before he remembered Asfal saying he had to be brave. He swallowed his tears, lifted his head, and walked quickly on to keep pace with Willow and Connor.

At the base of a broad, shallow staircase going up rather than down, Nessus halted and lifted a wing. His eagle eye rested on Rowan.

Something passed between the prince and the gryphon, and Beron wished for the hundredth time he could hear what it was. It mustn't have been polite, because Theia tsked and Willow frowned before telling Beron, 'We meet Lord Gryphon here, and we're to go up the stairs one at a time.' She paused.

'Rowan will go first because he carries Celeste, then me. You'll follow Connor.'

Beron worked it out. 'I'm to go last because I'm a Madach, and the least trustworthy because I have no magic in me. Despite Connor wearing a collar which makes Nessus believe him a traitor. Am I right?'

Willow patted his arm, smiled. 'Don't worry. Hold your head high and show them you're brave. You're the son of Tristan, Lord of Etting and friend to Danae, Sleih and Gryphon. It'll be fine, you'll see.'

She left his side, followed Rowan up the stairs. Beron fell in behind Connor. He couldn't help the faster pattering of his heart as he joined his new friends in Lord Gryphon's throne room. High-ceilinged, lit by burning torches, and warmed by a great, square firepit which glowed with a faintly greenish glow, it was the richest room they had seen.

And made richer by the presence of the regal gryphon sitting upright on his golden haunches. His glossy black wings shone in the torchlight, which also reflected in his stern brown gaze. Theia and Nessus moved to sit on either side of him.

Lord Gryphon lifted his foreleg, like a greeting. After a short silence (to Beron anyway), Rowan dropped to one knee and held Celeste out as an offering. Willow curtsied. Connor knelt. All three bowed their heads. Beron copied them, trying to appear confident, as if he was familiar with what was happening.

'Lord Gryphon,' Rowan said from his kneeling position. 'We come as friends of Asfal, your kin, and as the grandchildren of Ieldon, King of the Sleih.'

A pause before Rowan said, 'A wicked Lady, once a Seer of the Sleih, has woken the Evil which lay sleeping for centuries beneath the rocks of Asfarlon. Her army of white monsters has laid siege to the Citadel of Ilatias.' He glanced at Willow. Her head was still bowed. Rowan carried on. 'My sister and I escaped to rescue these two–' he lifted a hand from Celeste's hilt to wave at Beron and Connor '–who were her hostages. In the rescue, Asfal was injured. I think he was leading us here when the monsters attacked us the second time. Your Hunters rescued us.' He looked at Theia and Nessus. 'We hope you'll be able to help us return to Ilatias.'

Lord Gryphon's third eyelid flickered as he scrutinised first Rowan, then Willow, and Connor.

His gaze rested longest on the Danae. Lord Gryphon raised his foreleg. Flutters of anxiety tickled Beron's stomach. Would this magnificent gryphon strike Connor down because of the collar, which, he'd gathered although no one explained, worried Nessus and Theia? He stole a sideways, fearful look at his friend.

Connor flinched. The collar disappeared, leaving behind a faint sharp scent like old, cold ashes. Its presence was marked by red spots and welts which must have hurt and itched.

'Thank you, Lord Gryphon.' Connor stretched his neck in a slow circle, rubbing its raw redness.

'Thank you,' Willow said, and to Connor, 'The healers will have ointment for your skin. It'll be as good as new by tomorrow.'

Lord Gryphon shifted his study to Beron. Beron's cheeks heated. He ducked his head. If the stone floor opened up and swallowed him, he'd be happy.

'Beron is the son of Tristan, Lord of Etting,' Willow said. 'Tristan is a Gryphon friend. He disobeyed his own father to help Asfal and Callie drive the Madach invaders out of the Forest, and rescue the Danae from being enslaved.'

Beron's heart sank. Lord Gryphon would understand how brave Beron's father was, and how Beron could never live up to such bravery. Even when he tried, he was never good enough. From when he let the lady kidnap him – too easily – right up to today when he'd been no use at all fighting the monsters, he had failed to do anything worthwhile. He'd been a scared little boy, holding the princess's hand. He gulped down a rising, ashamed sob, clamping his lips together hard to stop it escaping and showing how pitiful he was. The others, with their magic and their truly brave spirits, would always be much more use than he could ever be.

Lord Gryphon paced slowly towards Beron. His eyes remained stern, and the anxious queasiness in Beron's stomach returned. What would this majestic gryphon do with him, a small boy with no magic in him, not a sliver? And a coward as well.

Look at me, Beron.

The voice sounded in Beron's head. He frowned. He'd imagined it. Wishful thinking. Yet, he slowly raised his head and looked.

Lord Gryphon peered at Beron as if he was a tasty morsel he might consider devouring. Beron trembled. His stomach heaved and his mind whirled with a kaleidoscope of images – himself in the schoolroom at home, not listening to his kind tutor; in the stable yard stealing away on his pony; and on the big black flying horse, scared witless and shivering as the lady flew him further and further from his parents, his tutor, his life in Etting. And in the cavern, petrified, his pitiful attempts to help Connor … and the attacks by the monsters, with nothing to fight the horrible creatures except his shouts and futile hand-waving. No weapon, no magic, worthless. All he had experienced since the lady took him swirled in his head like a maddened whirlpool. Dizziness, and shame, threatened to tumble him to the floor.

Lord Gryphon blinked. *You must learn, Beron, that true bravery is overcoming fear and doing what is right. A lesson your father learned.* He laid the giant talons of one leg gently on Beron's shoulder. *'You are a brave boy for one so young. Your heart and head tell me you value justice and honesty, and perhaps are too honest with yourself. I name you a worthy Gryphon friend.*

He lifted the talons and stood before Beron. His eyes were less stern.

Worthy? Brave? Lord Gryphon had spied into the depths of Beron's mind and soul and … and … said he was a worthy Gryphon friend? It couldn't be real. Beron's head threatened to float off his shoulders. There was something else odd about what Lord Gryphon said.

Beron's heart slammed into his ribs.

Lord Gryphon hadn't made his pronouncement out loud. He couldn't. What Beron heard was Lord Gryphon talking to Beron's mind. He had heard a gryphon speak.

The threatened tears changed from shame to joy. Beron let them come.

Gryphon friend!

Chapter Twenty Four

A warning

Captain Jarrow drove his new soldiers hard on their journey east. A late winter mildness gave rise to a thaw, and Isa's horse squelched along forest trails glutinous with mud. Snow would have been easier and cleaner. The snarling, loathsome beasts trailing them among the trees raised goosebumps on her skin. She desperately wished she didn't have to be on this journey. Drawing her cloak closer, Isa fingered her ring on its chain beneath her dress. The soft warmth she had felt when the Blue Lady came to make her demands had returned with the arrival of Jarrow and his monsters. This sliver of Sleih magic reassured her and gave her courage, a contrast to the cold pressure of the tension from her own people weighing heavily as she rode.

They muttered this was a mistake. Those abominable creatures would kill the Danae, not be any use capturing them. They begged Isa to tell Jarrow he didn't need his fearsome monsters. They would be enough.

Isa told him as they sat at their supper one snowy evening.

'You have no clue about these Danae, like I do.' Jarrow sneered, tossing into the fire a gnawed bone fished from the stew pot. 'They have witches, and while I'm promised there's none right now, I don't want to find out she's wrong.'

Isa understood 'she' to be the Blue Lady. She puzzled over how the shabby, uncouth Jarrow had come to be the companion of the elegant, evil witch. She didn't intend to ask. There was no love lost between them. Besides, her thoughts were taken up with how to turn things around when they reached the villages.

The air slipped back to its winter iciness. The horses slid on treacherous, frozen muddy ruts. The robbers cursed. They complained loudly that this raid could have waited until spring and it had better be worth it. Jarrow ignored them, spurring his horse on, forcing Isa and her people to do the same or lose their guide in the silent, trackless wood.

They camped at dusk beside an ice-choked stream where a thin rivulet of water escaped between snowy boulders. After finally coaxing a smoky fire from damp wood, Isa sat on her saddle beside it, eating a tepid, meagre supper. The robbers squatted in a circle around their own equally poor fire, spooning food into their mouths. Close by, their hobbled horses nosed in the slush, searching out any shoots of greenery.

Jarrow slouched on a fur-covered log, his boots stretched to the sputtering flames. 'Be there tomorrow,' he said. 'Our captives are close.' He waved to the east, where a hill rose to block the winter stars. 'Go in at dawn. Take the first village, the bigger one, lock 'em up in their fancy Elders' hall and the inn. After that, the second one, straight off, before anyone can raise an alarm.' He grinned, yellow teeth lit by the fire contrasting with the greying ginger of his unkempt beard.

Isa's pulse raced. Dawn? She had until dawn to warn Gwen and Lucy? Her thoughts raced.

'I'll tell my men.' She stood, waved at the low tent which was her shelter each night. 'And then sleep. I need my rest. We'll be ready before dawn.'

Jarrow pulled out the bottle he carried inside his heavy coat, raised it to her in a grinning salute. Isa walked towards her people, listening to the bottle's stopper pulled and the captain's noisy gulps. She hoped he would drink as he normally did. It was unlikely he'd be awake before dawn, but she couldn't count on it.

***

Gwen poked the reluctant flames in the tiny parlour's fireplace in the cottage where she grew up and where she had lived alone since her mother's passing. 'Bed, or more wood, and we sit longer in the warmth?'

Verian, curled in Gwen's spare cushioned chair, grinned. 'I vote for being warm. Besides, you won't sleep. You never do.'

Gwen apologised for her disturbed nights, which had her pacing the cottage at all hours.

Verian waved away the apology. 'I understand,' she said. 'No word from the Citadel, not knowing whether Connor and Beron are safe, or where Melda is or what she's doing.'

Gwen curled in her chair, drawing a woollen shawl around her shoulders. 'I hate what this is doing to Lucy.' She fingered the shawl's tassels, thinking about the scene in her sister's home earlier in the evening.

Lucy begged each day for news, which Gwen couldn't give her. Tonight, Lucy had scoffed. 'Callie can't send her owl to us? Has she forgotten us entirely?'

'Of course not.' Gwen hated this snappy, irritable Lucy. 'There must be a reason.'

'No good reason.' Peter continued sharpening a spade, which, along with a heavy iron mallet he used in the mill, were the best he could find for weapons. His brow was constantly furrowed. He grew older than his years, more stooped, every day.

Lucy fell into a kitchen chair, put her head in her hands, and moaned. Gwen had stroked her sister's hair, murmured consoling nonsense which Lucy ignored, before letting herself out and returning to her guest. Gwen's heart ached for Connor's parents, as well as for herself.

She had another reason for her sleeplessness. No real defences had been put in place in case Melda attacked. Matthew and a handful of like-minded villagers had a plan for hurriedly sending the old, the children, and those unable to fight into hiding. They stockpiled blankets and food in two far barns, packaged to make them easy to carry into the deeper forest. The few horses and oxen owned by farmers ready to err on the side of caution were taken there each evening, stabled along with the cows.

They could possibly send people into hiding at short notice.

As for defending their homes, to drive off Melda and whatever force she brought with her – nothing had been done. Elder James insisted there was no need, what quarrel did this lady have with the Danae? All stuff and nonsense, he claimed.

In her firelit parlour, Gwen made a decision. 'I have to return to the Citadel, find out what's happening. I'll go tomorrow.' She clasped her hands, looked at Verian. 'If you'll stay here, help Matthew and the others, fight with him if needed?'

'Of course—'

Banging interrupted her. Gwen jumped up, flew across the room, and hauled the door wide.

'Matthew? Has something …? And who…?' She stood on tiptoes, squinting into the night. She gasped. 'Isa? Is it you?'

'One of the lads found her on the track near the mill.' Matthew laid his hand on Isa's shoulder. She shrugged it off irritably. Gwen's lips tugged into a tiny smile. 'Said she had to see you, Lucy, or Mark, and it was life and death urgent.' Matthew tipped his head at Isa's untidy red curls. 'You recognise her?'

'Come in, come in.' Gwen ushered her visitors inside. 'What by the Beings are you doing here, Isa? How did you find us?' She waved at the chair she'd vacated. 'Sit, sit,' and to Matthew she said, 'It's all right, Isa's an old friend, from beyond the Deep Forest.'

Isa didn't sit. She clenched her fists. 'A man, a Madach captain, Jarrow—'

'Jarrow?' Gwen's hands went to her mouth. 'What about him?'

'The Blue Lady,' Isa said. 'She came to the camp, promised we could have our Danae fairytale slaves and she'd send this captain to show us the way, help capture you all—'

'Jarrow's with Melda?'

'Wasn't he the one tried to enslave you all before?' Verian asked.

'Yes.' Gwen took hold of Isa's cold, calloused hand. 'Isa saved me and Mark, more than once.' She frowned. 'Is Chester still your leader? Does he still want us?'

'No. I'm their leader, for what it's worth.'

Gwen winced at her bitterness.

'The Blue Lady spoke to me, but this–' Isa reached inside the top of her dress and drew out a ring on a chain '–stopped her seeing inside my head, like she can do. Like what addled poor Chester's brains.'

Gwen recognised the jewel. No ordinary ring, it must carry Gryphon magic. King Ieldon's foresight might save them again. 'And you've come to warn us?' she said. 'That Jarrow might attack?'

Isa shook her head, red curls flying. 'Not might. He's here, camped over the hill, saying he's gonna attack the villages at dawn.'

'Here? Dawn?' Matthew strode to the door, opened it. The low flames on the fire bent in protest at the cold wind. 'I'll go to Peter,' he said to Gwen. 'Tell him those who're leaving need to get away immediately. You go to the other village and send them to the barns.' He stepped into the night, calling, 'Rouse Elder James and bring him to the inn. I'll meet you there.' He was gone, slamming the door behind him.

Verian yanked on her boots and threw her cloak around her. 'I'll bring the wolves to the inn. Tell the villagers not to fear them.'

As Verian left, Gwen lifted Isa's cold hand to her own warm cheek. 'Saved again, thank you.'

'Let's hope so,' Isa muttered, taking back her hand. 'You ought to know though, it's not Jarrow and my people by themselves.' She scowled at the door. 'Your friends should've stayed long enough to let me tell 'em about the monsters.'

***

Gwen's first task was to waken the sleepers in the smaller village and have them spread the warning from house to house. Lucy arrived, dressed ready to help lead the refugees, and with warm hugs of gratitude to Isa. Leaving Lucy to carry on, Gwen and the robber leader climbed the winding, steep hill to Elder James' big cottage.

James was reluctant to leave his home and bed. Despite Isa's presence, he refused to believe Gwen's tale, moaning about old stories and too much imagination, and accusing Gwen of bringing strangers to his home to frighten him for fun. Isa quickly lost patience and shouted what a stupid man he was and if he didn't want to spend his days playing at being a fairytale butler to a Madach lord, he had better come along to the inn. James glowered at her fury, but grumpily gave in.

'This had better be worth waking the whole village for,' he grumbled before stalking to his bedroom to throw on warm clothes.

In the big village's square, lit by multiple torches, Matthew and Peter had gathered the elderly, the sick, children, and others who couldn't fight. Helped by a group of older women, the two men checked blankets, boots, and food. The crowd buzzed with anxious murmurs. Small children, woken rudely from sleep, cried and clung to their white-faced mothers who soothed them, exclaiming it was an adventure and they needed to be brave. Old people stood silently, waiting to be told what to do. A few who were ill lay on pallets held off the slushy cobbles by friends or family.

Gwen bit her lip. The group would be slow, they had a long way to go, and the middle of a winter night was the worst time to be trekking through a forest. She took solace from her own venture in among the trees a few days before. Unlike Callie, Gwen could not hear the Forest creatures' thoughts. Over the years, however, as she gathered leaves, mushrooms, roots, and flowers for her healing potions, they had come to accept her. Wanting to ensure her medicines were fresh and plentiful if needed, she and Verian had gone in search of berries and other winter growing plants, digging in the snow at the base of trees to find what they could.

'Look,' Verian had said, moving only her eyes to show Gwen the circle of animals watching them.

Slowly, Gwen turned to face them, and, feeling more than a little silly, said softly, 'Yes, trouble might be coming, and we'll need your help. You remember, even if the villagers don't.'

The wild creatures had slipped into the Forest, singly and

in groups. She left with a lighter heart, certain the foxes, the bigger birds, the boar, the deer would keep the Danae safe among them.

And there were the trees too, those seeded by ancient beech, oak, willow and other giants which marched from Callie's Secret Valley to replant the Forest after Jarrow's mindless destruction. The trees had responded to her plea too, their boughs gently waving as if to assure Gwen they were aware, they were on the side of the Danae. They would offer protection beyond mere shelter.

James interrupted her thoughts. He had stopped walking to watch the scene in the square. 'What's going on?' he said to Gwen.

'As we tried to tell you a thousand times, we wanted to make sure those who couldn't fight would be safe. We're sending them into the Forest to hide.'

'In this weather?' James's caterpillar eyebrows arched. 'They'll freeze.'

'No,' Matthew said. 'They're prepared for the cold. It's all planned.'

'Ah. Prepared, hey?' James rubbed his lip. He held up his hand. 'Villagers,' he called. 'I am here, your Senior Elder. Be assured.'

The villagers quieted. Would James encourage his people, give them hope as they set off, not knowing what they would return to?

'I will go with you,' he said. 'I will personally lead you into exile to ensure your safety.'

Go with them? A surge of anger rose in Gwen's throat. She rounded on James.

'Your role is here, defending their homes,' she hissed. 'Not running into hiding.'

Others apparently shared her view. No-one cheered or clapped. They muttered and turned away as if embarrassed.

'They have excellent leaders, James.' Matthew indicated the women who had ignored the Senior Elder to continue checking everyone was ready to leave. 'Mara, Ruth, and Ellen well understand the plans we've made. They helped make them.' Glancing at Gwen, who nodded, he said, 'Lucy's already at the other village, making sure they're prepared. They don't need your help.' He held James' shifting gaze while gesturing at the inn, where men, women and older boys and girls carrying shovels, rakes, forks, and pokers trailed into the brightly lit room. 'In there is where you belong, showing your face to those of us left behind to fight Jarrow's men.'

James scowled. He scanned the crowd, likely hoping for someone to plead how desperately they needed him. No one spoke.

Gwen's anger subsided. She could have been sorry for the Elder until Isa spoke up.

'Jarrow don't have his own men, only mine,' she said to Matthew. 'I tried to tell you before, at Gwen's, when you left in such a hurry.' She waved her hand sharply when he opened his mouth to speak. 'Don't get excited though,' she said. 'This captain has worse than men with him.'

'Worse than men?' James's scowl deepened. 'What are you talking about, whoever you are?'

'What do you mean?' Gwen said, more gently.

'Monsters.' Isa stood straight, clenched her fists at her side. 'Seems the Blue Lady created 'em out of real animals, maybe even people.' She shuddered. 'White fur, white skin, red or yellow eyes what glow at night. Always hungry, and all with claws and teeth to make you dread turning your back if they're anywhere near.'

The silence lasted two heartbeats. Matthew broke it. He punched the air. 'Get out of here. Go!' he shouted to the waiting villagers. 'And don't return until you're told it's safe.'

Gwen's skin crawled, imagining the terrible force waiting to attack them. Safe? Would they ever be safe?

Chapter Twenty Five

The gryphons learn a lesson

A fierce, gusty wind which had risen during the night blustered against the leather curtain across the opening to the ledge outside. Despite cold draughts snaking around the billowing leather, the glowing firepit filled the cave with warmth.

Willow sat cross-legged on furs with Connor, Rowan and Beron beside a table bearing the remains of breakfast. Her night had been restless, worried about Asfal, anxious about what was happening in the Citadel and how desperate her mother must be, not knowing if she and Rowan were safe. Or alive.

'Is there any word about Asfal?' Connor asked, nibbling at the last mushroom.

'The healers have moved him and he's sleeping,' Willow said.

She had wandered the halls in the grey dawn searching for him until an early rising gryphon guided her to the hospital, a long, narrow cavern with two rows of sweetly scented beds of meadow hay either side of a wide passage.

'They won't say if the wing will heal fully.' The idea Asfal might not fly sickened Willow. She rested her arms on the table, head bent.

'He'll heal.' Beron's stubborn optimism cheered her, mostly because it showed how far his own recovery had come.

'Why did Asfal never tell us,' Rowan said, 'about Lord Gryphon?'

Willow humphed. 'Why did Grandfather never tell us?' She grimaced. 'Quite a shock when Lord Gryphon sent his greetings to his old friend Ieldon, and knew who you and I were.'

'Like the days before Jarrow came to the Forest,' Connor said, 'when the Sleih and Danae each believed the other to be a myth, a fairytale from long ago. It seems legends come to life all the time.'

'One thing Father did tell me,' Beron said, 'was how surprised they all were at finding Danae in the Forest.' He moved to the broad straw-heaped bed where the four of them had spent a scratchy, although warm, night, and bent to tug on his boots, dried by the fire. 'And more surprised to find out about the Sleih.'

'Legend or not–' Rowan stretched, yawned '–I hope Lord Gryphon decides soon what he's going to do with us.' He glanced at the heavily rustling curtain, and shivered. 'We can't walk home, not until spring anyway. And who knows what will have happened by that time?'

Willow stood, staring at the arch into the hallway. 'I can't abide this waiting–'

You will be pleased then not to have to wait longer. Golden-feathered Theia came into the cave. She ruffled her wings impatiently. *Lord Gryphon wishes to speak with you all.*

Willow looked at Beron, who grinned. She shared his excitement, knowing he could hear Theia's words as clearly as she could.

'What will happen?' Connor asked.

Lord Gryphon has not yet decided.

Which is all Theia would say as she led them to what Willow had learned was called the Council Room. The same as in the Citadel.

Lord Gryphon was not alone this time. He sat on a deep, black pelt flanked by several gryphons. Theia, as leader of the Hunters, joined them at one end. This must be the Council, Willow assumed. Although the gryphons' thoughts were shielded, they couldn't disguise the coolness with which they regarded Willow and her companions.

The Council has listened to your story, Lord Gryphon said, *and have debated long into the night.* He lifted his wings, settled them. *We are of different opinions about whether we should offer help in this matter.*

Willow clenched her jaw. Beside her, Rowan stiffened and Celeste swung slightly in its scabbard.

A gryphon of great age, judging by the streaks of grey in his deep purple feathers, bobbed his head. *The tale of the Fall of Asfarlon, when the gryphon pendant was forged to defeat the Evil, has been kept alive among Gryphon-kind. Have you heard of the pendant?*

'You know more about this than I do,' Rowan said to Willow.

'Yes.' Willow concentrated on the old gryphon. 'The pendant was found, not long ago, and is kept safe in the Citadel. Hasn't Grandfather, I mean, King Ieldon, told you this?'

No. Perhaps he didn't consider it important. Lord Gryphon's tone suggested perhaps also his friend Ieldon had made an error of judgement.

'She wants the pendant,' Connor blurted. 'This Lady Melda, the Seer.'

'She mustn't have it,' Willow said. 'Grandfather says it'd be disastrous.'

Why hasn't it been used to stop her, as it was by Ilesse and Queen Gweyr to defeat the Evil?

'I think ...' Willow rubbed her chin, remembering the conversation she'd overhead when Beron's father and Gwen rushed to the Citadel wanting help to find the boys. 'Its powers have faded. It's been a long, long time since it was made.'

The Council of gryphons hooded their eyes, turning their great eagle heads to each other as if in conversation. Willow shifted her feet. Rowan fiddled with the hilt of Celeste, and Connor and Beron stared about the cavern, wide-eyed at the splendour of the wall hangings, the thickness of the furs on the floor.

Why should we involve ourselves in this fight? The grey-streaked gryphon spoke. *The last time we came between the Sleih and this Evil, our voices were ripped from our throats and our ancient home destroyed.*

Involve themselves? 'We're not asking you to do anything,' Willow said, 'except take us home to Ilatias.'

Except? A gryphon with feathers of deepest green snapped her mighty beak. Willow jumped. *How can we help in any way without this Seer, and likely the Evil which hangs on her, learning of our existence?* She shook out her wings, irritated. *And once aware, you think she, it, will not desire our magic, our power? To invade our minds, take us over?*

'Oh.' Willow grew hot. Of course. Such an abundance of Gryphon magic would imbue Melda with powers which the Evil would twist and tease into a terrible, destructive force.

You understand our hesitation, Lord Gryphon said. The councillors bobbed their great eagle heads in agreement.

'Is it because you're afraid?' Beron stepped forward, fists clenched at his side. His cheeks were flushed.

Theia's head jerked up. *Afraid? Gryphons are not cowards.*

Lord Gryphon shushed her with a quick lift of one wing. He eyed Beron as he might a puppy which had scratched him in play.

'Excuse me saying so, please, Lord.' Beron stumbled on. 'Yesterday you told me true bravery is beating fear and doing what's right.' His face grew redder. 'I don't mean to be impolite, I'm sorry …'

A cold silence descended in the cavern. Willow sneaked a glance at the green gryphon, who had twisted her head to fix Beron with a baleful eye. Willow's pulse jumped in her neck. The boy had upset them all. They would be forced to spend winter in these caverns, doing nothing, their families believing them dead. And afterwards, they would need to attempt a long, treacherous journey to reach whatever might be left of Ilatias. She clasped her hands, her nails digging into her palms. Stupid Beron.

The boy is right. Lord Gryphon faced the row of councillors, first on one side, then the other. *He quotes me exactly. Shame on us to be forced to see the truth in our own words.*

Willow unclenched her hands.

The gryphons shifted on their pelts, looked to the high ceiling, across to the firepit, and along the walls. The green gryphon alone appeared unmoved, staring angrily at Beron.

Willow waited. Beron's cheeks blazed. Rowan stopped fiddling with the sword hilt, and Connor stood, legs planted apart, chewing his bottom lip.

The old gryphon spoke first. *If this Seer takes on the power of the Evil, she will discover us soon enough. Do we skulk in our caverns, hoarding our magic, pretending nothing is amiss?*

Giving us time to prepare, the green gryphon muttered.

Lord Gryphon stood, claws and talons firm on the black pelt. *Or do we go to the aid of those who were once like kin to us?* He scanned the councillors' faces. *Do we have the courage to fight for what is right, take this Evil head on while it is yet unaware of us?*

Of course we have the courage. Theia's commanding tone rang in Willow's head.

The councillors fluffed their wings, blinked. Willow caught snatches of their thoughts, and her heart lifted.

'Yes, the little boy is right,' and *'Once we had common cause with the Sleih, we should again.'* There were a few silences, not all convinced.

Lord Gryphon took a step closer to Beron, and peered down, head tilted to the side. *Thank you for the lesson, Gryphon friend,* he said.

Beron's hot cheeks shone like the coals in the firepit.

***

'Sirs.' Connor raised his hand as if he was in the schoolroom at home. He lowered his hand and concentrated on what he needed to say.

Most of the Gryphon councillors had left the cavern, including Theia, who hurried out saying she would prepare her Hunters. The green gryphon had stalked out with no word to anyone that Connor heard.

The old purple gryphon remained. *Yes?* he said to Connor.

'Sirs, I don't come from the Citadel. I'm from beyond the Deep Forest of Arneithe, where the Danae live by the oceans.' He stopped, remembering these gryphons had not heard of his people.

You must explain about the Danae, Lord Gryphon said. *For now, it's enough we hear the thrum of Sleih blood in your veins and see the spark of magic, unschooled and raw, which glimmers in your soul.*

'Umm, yes, of course.' Connor had a more urgent mission than telling old stories. 'You see, Lady Melda wants to sell the Danae into slavery, pretending to the Madach in distant lands we're a fairytale people.' He threw up his hands. 'I need to go home, please, if I can. To warn them, or ... or ...' The notion there might not be anyone left to warn lodged like a stone in his gut. How much time had passed since Melda made her threats, promising Jarrow he could have his slaves? He had no idea, except it was long enough for her to have descended on the villagers with her misshapen, terrifying creatures. His stomach clenched.

Lord Gryphon peered at him. Connor sensed the stately gryphon reading the dread in his mind. *I see,* the gryphon said.

The purple gryphon raised a wing. *My son, Nessus, carried this boy here. He was impressed by his bravery fighting this lady's monsters, and by his quick grasp of his latent magic.*

Hmm. Lord Gryphon blinked at his councillor. *Then Nessus shall carry him home. He will be his guardian, aid him in whatever fight he must endure.*

'Can I go with them?' Beron took a step closer to Connor. 'Please? I'd be more use there than at the Citadel where there's lots of soldiers and people who can fight. I could help Connor.' He straightened his shoulders, set his face in what Connor assumed was meant to be a fierce, fighting expression.

'Or you could stay here,' Willow said firmly. 'And when it's safe, we can send you to Etting, to your mother and father.'

Beron's jaw hung in horror. 'And tell Father I waited out this war – because it is a war – in hiding?' His voice rose on the last word.

Willow flinched.

Connor grinned. 'If Nessus will carry two of us, please come with me.' His grin fell away. 'If it's all gone wrong, I'll need a friend.'

Chapter Twenty Six

Wolves and monsters

The wan light of morning barely lit a heavy fog when Jarrow rolled out of his tent. He cursed Isa for not waking him earlier.

'Not my place,' she told him, sipping at her hot, aromatic drink. Gwen had pressed the packet of leaves into her hands when Isa left the Danae in pre-dawn blackness. It would keep her awake, give her strength for the day.

Isa would need strength. As would the Danae.

'Your lot ready?' Jarrow glowered at the fire where Isa's people sat waiting, their horses saddled.

'Yes.' Isa swallowed a response about being ready since dawn. In truth, she would have waited longer, given her friends more time to prepare themselves, and for the refugees to put as much distance as possible between themselves and the white monsters.

The icy fog refused to lift, shrouding their way to the villages. More than once, Jarrow swore and doubled back on his tracks. Isa sent a prayer of thanks for this new delay. Then the white monsters caught the scent of prey – prey which wasn't denied them as Isa and her fellows were. They wove in swift, deadly silence between the trees, leaving barely a paw or claw print in the frozen snow.

Isa spurred her horse alongside Jarrow. 'They'll get there long before us and kill everyone,' she said. She hoped her panic would be taken for loss of slaves, not terror at the fate of her friends.

The robbers grumbled their agreement, pointing out this was exactly what they said would happen and why were these gross creatures here anyway?

Jarrow halted, stood awkwardly in his stirrups and called to his army. 'Alive, remember, alive! You will have your reward as your mistress promised.'

The monsters slowed, sniffing, their red and yellow eyes seeking out Jarrow. He thrust out his chest. 'Like proper-trained hunting dogs, they are. See? Promise of a treat to come and they'll eat out of your hand.'

Reward? Treat to come? A sudden, awful, thought hit Isa. What was this reward? Once the Danae were captured and bound, her people were of no further use to Jarrow. Or the Blue Lady. Nausea choked her. She gagged. What stupidity had led her to agree to this? The Blue Lady had tricked her with her wicked games. Isa hated the Blue Lady with all her soul.

They came at last to the forest track which ran alongside the fields, past the mill and forge to the larger of the two villages. The fog hid all from view. Isa concentrated on the stony road. Ahead, the monsters stalked silently, snouts and noses lifted, sniffing. She waited for a challenge from the Danae. Hadn't they set guards on the tracks?

All remained quiet, except the snorting of the horses and jangling of harness. And Isa's heart thumping loud enough for the world to hear.

'Wolves!' shrieked a robber.

'Aagghh!' Others yelled their own fear.

Screams rose from Isa's people. A line of grey and black wolves emerged from the fog. They came along the track from the village, slowly, deliberately, heads thrust forward, teeth bared.

A tall woman wrapped in a long leather cloak walked behind them. Her straight black hair flowed past her shoulders like a river at midnight. She held a wooden staff upright. Isa shivered at the mystical sight of her and her wolves, despite knowing this was Verian, the Danae Queen of the Caverns.

The robbers' horses reared in panic, snorting and whinnying. Isa's horse too. She struggled to calm the beast, remembering

Verian's promise the wolves would harm neither the horses or the Madach – barring Jarrow if they could get to him. Their enemy were the monsters which, with no word from Jarrow, hurled themselves at the wolves.

Verian raised her staff, and the pack leaped to meet the attack. Isa's stomach rebelled at the clash of snarling, baying, creatures. Jarrow drove his wide-eyed, high-stepping horse nearer the fighting, screaming encouragement.

The robbers gained control of their mounts, and sat panting, mouths agape, staring at the melee of twisting bodies, at the blood-spattered snow.

'Take them!'

Isa jumped at the command, which came from behind her. Her people turned, bringing their horses around, searching for the voice ... or voices ...

Out of the rising fog, Danae brandishing pitchforks, rakes, and shovels ran from the trees towards the robbers.

Except one. This man ran forward briefly, slowed until he was at the back of the villagers, circled an oak and, crouched low over his large belly, disappeared into the Forest. Isa gritted her teeth. Elder James. He was a worse leader of his people than she was.

She forgot him, turning her attention to where Matthew, Peter and Gwen led the villagers onto the track, trapping the robbers on their twisting, whinnying horses between themselves and the blood-tingling battle. Yelling, waving razor-edged makeshift weapons, they forced herself and her robbers nearer the frenzied fighting.

Not only Danae.

Wild boar as solid as boulders lined up either side of the villagers. Mighty tusks waving, the boar galloped through the panicking Madach to charge into the fray against the monsters.

The robbers' jaws dropped, disbelieving.

'Witchcraft,' Jarrow screamed. He shook his fist at the boar. 'She promised me, she said ...'

Two wide-winged eagles, talons stretched, fell from the foggy sky into the battle. The Madach cried their fear into the fog.

'Witchcraft?' 'The woman in the cloak. She's a witch.' 'Demons and magic, we can't fight that.'

'Isa,' a voice called, trembling in fear. 'Tell 'em we surrender.'

Others took up the call. 'Yes, we give up,' and 'We don't want no Danae.'

'No.' Jarrow's roar cut across the robbers' babbled protests. He gestured at the Danae, standing with their weapons, cutting off any Madach retreat. 'Bind 'em! Here's your chance.'

Three robbers drove their horses to attack the villagers. The Danae lifted their weapons, shouting defiance. Wolves with bloodied fur and red teeth came from nowhere, rearing up at the attackers, snapping and growling.

'Don't hurt them, please,' Isa whispered.

The three Madach hauled on their reins, although their horses needed no signal to stop. They pranced sideways, away from the wolves and the Danae. The riders let them.

The rest of Isa's people huddled in a knot, the battling creatures behind them, the Danae and more wolves in front. Isa, calming her horse, searched for Matthew, and found him. Please help, she mouthed silently.

Matthew held up his hand. The Danae quieted.

'Leave us,' he called to the Madach. 'Return to your camp, or suffer the fury of the Danae and the creatures of the Forest.'

'Stay!' Jarrow wheeled his horse to face Isa. His face behind his ratty beard glowed red with fury. 'Command them to stay, to capture their slaves. They're your people, tell 'em they have no choice.'

Isa gazed across the group of trembling robbers. 'You can leave.' She had to shout above the snarls and howling of the creatures. She called to Verian, who stood watching her wolves battle the monsters. 'Will you let them pass with no harm?'

'Yes,' Verian murmured. She raised her staff and the wolves protecting the villagers weaved through the panicked Madach to rejoin the fighting.

'Matthew?' Isa called.

Matthew signalled yes, and the Danae parted. The Madach spurred their willing horses into the gap and fled along the track to the forge and mill. Jarrow's curses followed them like a demonic challenge.

'You, Isa?' Matthew said.

'Nah.' She grinned at him. 'I have a deal with–'

'Watch out!' Matthew ran forward.

Jarrow had spurred his horse and bore down on Isa. A knife glinted in his upraised hand. Matthew grabbed for the bridle of Isa's horse. He missed.

'Traitor!' The knife flashed.

Chapter Twenty Seven

Melda's poison

The night guard slept, exhausted by their efforts to clear the Citadel's walls of Melda's creeping reptiles. Callie opened the door to her haggard brother, who hungrily spooned up watery porridge while telling her how the reptiles grew in number and speed.

'The Seers spend their time running from one place to the next, burning them from the walls,' he said.

'The iron? Has it been tested?'

'Yes.' Mark pushed the empty bowl aside. 'We daren't waste arrows, not yet, but one grotesque creature came too close to the parapet.' His smile was grim. 'A young guard attacked it with an iron-tipped spear, and it did as you said – died at the touch.'

'They keep coming though?'

'Melda appears to have an unlimited supply.' Mark folded his arms across his creased, dirty tunic. 'Elrane argues we need to attack, soon. Ieldon agrees. It's the Council slowing things. They plead for enough weapons to be made to arm every able body in the Citadel.' He lifted his eyebrows. 'Including those who might have no choice but to defend themselves.'

Callie's heart skipped a beat, her mind filling with the nightmare of those creatures flooding the Citadel, devouring young, old ... anyone in their path. The King's Tower could hold, for a time. Ieldon, however, would never abandon his people to face such an awful fate alone.

Callie sent Mark to sleep and, restless, left the house. The grey, windswept day with black clouds roiling above the Citadel matched her heavy heart as she walked the deserted streets to the palace. The iron gates stood open. Within the walls the king's servants gave out small loaves of bread, squares of cheese, rice, and dried meat wrapped in paper. There was nothing fresh to eat. Sleih and Madach alike queued quietly under the eyes of four Seers, taking their small parcels and walking rapidly away. There was no need for guards, who were either resting or on the battlements.

Looking up, Callie saw the king and the prince had joined the guards and Seers defending the walls. Ieldon paused to touch each Seer on the forehead, passing his own magic to bolster theirs. The prince stood beside the guards, his attention fixed on the walls and at the heaving, dirty white mass spread across the fields.

Climbing the stone stairway, Callie passed through the low door onto the walkway. A burst of green flames rose from the outer wall. The Seer who had cast the fire staggered, righted himself, and pressed his hand against the inner parapet, slumped with weariness. Callie quickened her pace. She could not cast fire, but she could offer her own magic to help the Seers who could. Before she reached the Seer, however, a force, like a cold hand squeezing her brain, held her fast. She battled the force, drawing up a shield like a drawbridge, and slowly turned to the outer wall.

'Ieldon! I have news.' Melda's screech pierced Callie's head, as it must have pierced all who were nearby.

The king strode to the parapet and peered over. Callie and Prince Elrane joined him, ready to bolster his magic to stop any mind-meddling the Seer wished to play at.

'Ah, the little witch is here, I see. Good.'

Melda drew out the word 'good' with smiling pleasure. Callie knew, in that instant, there was fresh grief to bear.

'What is it you wish to say, Melda? We have nothing to say to you, except be gone from our walls.'

'Oh dear, Ieldon.' The lady adopted a flirtatious tone. 'Don't be grumpy. I'm being very patient.' She grinned, her teeth white against her golden skin. 'Your people must be hungry, and anxious for the precious children and the dear elderly who do not, I imagine, take well to hunger.'

She paused. Ieldon didn't respond.

'Cat got your tongue?' Melda laughed. 'My cats will enjoy your tongue, eventually.' She held her bronze rod high, the diamond glowing bright in the gloom of the morning. 'You wish to hear my news?'

Ieldon held his silence. Melda giggled. 'Such a strong man.' She plunged the rod deep into the black mud. The diamond swayed, steadied.

Callie made herself turn from the sight. All along the wall, guards stared at the white light, mesmerised.

'Elrane,' Callie whispered. 'The guards ...'

Elrane snapped his head back from where he too had been captured by the diamond's glow. Stiffly, as if it took great effort, he walked along the wall, touching each guard's shoulder, urging them around so they couldn't see the jewel.

'You will be distraught, little witch,' Melda called, 'to learn your family is in my tender care. Or at least, in the attentive care of my faithful captain. Captured, with the aid of those same robber Madach who desperately sought their fairytale slaves all those years ago.'

Callie's skin prickled. Melda had sent Jarrow to the Danae. As she feared, his lust for revenge would have made him eager. He had help from the robbers. Callie recalled Gwen telling her how these robbers captured them, more than once, and about their rescue by Verian's wolves one time, and by a badger calling for help another. Fun stories at the time. Not anymore.

'Is this true, Melda?' King Ieldon spoke calmly.

'Of course it's true,' she snapped. 'Dead, or on their way to slavery. The captain is delighted.'

Callie choked on her fury and sorrow. How would she tell Mark?

'And, you say, aided by the robber Madach?' the king asked.

'The one with the wild red hair. She's their leader.' The smirk in Melda's voice swelled Callie's anger. 'A simple task to tempt her to succeed where the men had failed before.'

The girl, Isa? Callie's anger bolstered her grief. She had thought Isa to be Gwen's friend. A treacherous one, it seemed.

'Ah, I see.' The king's calm reached out to Callie to soothe her fury.

She refused to be soothed. Striding to the wall, she placed her hands on the stone and cried out to her enemy.

'If one hair of their heads is harmed, you will pay doubly for it, Melda. I swear by the Beings, by Gryphon magic, your end will be painful and humiliating.'

Melda's cruel, joyless laughter split the air. 'A mere matter of time, Ieldon, and your family too will be mine to play with. Think on that!'

She waved the rod and vanished in a smoky, black cloud.

'Beware!' Elrane's commanding tone sent Callie stumbling away from the wall.

A reptile's head cast about where she had been standing, seeking prey. A Seer threw out her hands, throwing green fire at the beast. It fell, silently, to the mud. All along the wall more waving, bulbous heads rose above the stones. Seers and guards fought together to send the reptiles hurtling to the ground.

Callie, her eyes wet, gathered her loathing and her heartache into herself and followed after Ieldon as he moved from one Seer to the next, nurturing strength, murmuring courage.

The attack of the reptiles went on for a long time. Weak sunlight parted the clouds, casting a glimmering light on the white horde. The reptiles came, were repelled. The malformed bears, wolves, cats below yowled and bayed until the noise threatened to send Callie screaming to her rooms. Their rancid stink filled the air.

At last, a touch on Callie's shoulder. Mark stood there, refreshed and ready for the fight.

'Go home, rest,' he urged. He swept a hand along the walkway where a new guard and different Seers joined the battle.

Gratefully, Callie obeyed, not wanting to tell him, not yet, of Melda's victory, of the fate of Lucy, Gwen, Peter, and the villagers. Or of Isa's betrayal.

King Ieldon took Callie's arm and supported her down the rough stairs. In the courtyard, she stopped.

'The robber girl,' she said. 'Gwen and Mark spoke fondly of her and how she'd helped them.' She strangled the sobs rising up her throat. 'How could she betray them?' If Asfal was here, he and Callie could have travelled swiftly to the aid of the villagers. Tears welled. He was not, and to ride there would be too late, and would take the pendant into danger.

The king's tired eyes gazed into Callie's. 'We cannot trust a word the woman says.' He rubbed his sweaty forehead. 'Isa has a gift from us which once she treasured above all else. If she wears it, it will have protected her from Melda's mind games.' He laid a hand on Callie's aching shoulder. 'Hold your anger close. You will need it before this is over. Your grief, however, you should put aside until you are certain it is necessary.' He gave her his half-smile. 'Young Isa was a brave, smart, and loyal friend to your brother and sisters. I suspect she remains so.'

Callie took comfort. Ieldon understood people, and if he believed Isa remained loyal, she would willingly believe him. The alternative was unthinkable. However, whether or not Melda's claims were true, the Danae must be under attack by Jarrow. With nothing to defend themselves.

The king removed his hand and waved Callie in the direction of home. 'Rest. Tomorrow I will tell the Council we are as ready as we will ever be. Elrane is right. We must attack. Soon. Whatever the consequences.'

Chapter Twenty Eight

The fate of the Danae

Jarrow's knife plunged towards Isa. Gwen screamed. Matthew threw himself at the captain. Too late. The knife sank into Isa's shoulder.

Silently, she tipped sideways, falling from her horse. Matthew scrambled up, breaking her fall. He laid her on the trampled, slushy ground.

A grey wolf leapt at Jarrow. Flailing, unbalanced, he brandished his knife. The wolf halted, growling, and in that moment, a bloodied, mud-streaked monster threw itself against the wolf's side. Twisting, jaws open, the wolf sprang. The monster's shriek pierced Gwen's head like a nightmare before it fell to its side, lifeless.

Verian lifted her hand, palm up, and the wolf staggered to her, collapsing in a panting heap at her feet.

Ignoring Jarrow, Gwen bent over her friend, tearing at Isa's tunic to see the wound. Isa's eyes were open, frightened. Her skin was slick with sweat and her breath came in ragged gasps.

'It hurts.' She groaned, her eyelids fluttering. 'I'm going to die, aren't I?'

'No,' Gwen said. 'It's deep, but shoulders heal better than heads. Or hearts.' She tore off a strip from the hem of Isa's red-soaked top, bunched it and pressed it to the wound, while saying to Matthew, 'We need to take her to my house.' She jerked her head in the direction of the village and home. Monstrous creatures grappled with Verian's wolves and tusk-waving boar. They blocked the track, and a swathe of forest either side. 'We need to get past all that.'

Jarrow stood, legs splayed, the knife gripped in his hand. He stared at Peter who glared at him across the injured woman.

'Where's my son?' Peter shouted. 'Where's that evil woman taken him?'

'Your son?' Jarrow smirked. 'Red curls, green eyes, freckles?'

'Connor, his name is Connor. Where is he?'

'Don't fret. He was alive last I saw. Him and the other one.' Jarrow grinned. 'You might get him back … in one piece, though what she'll do to his mind …' He sighed deeply, as if in sorrow. 'Mind you–' he banished his pretend sadness with a genuine smirk '–it won't matter after my army here has done with this pack of wild animals, and you're all where you belong. My prisoners.'

Gwen stood beside Matthew who cradled the bleeding Isa in his arms. Nausea filled her stomach. Several of Verian's wolves lay wounded, or possibly worse, on the track. A boar limped into the trees. Gwen winced when it was set upon by white monsters. The boar found strength to swing its tusks, sending the monsters into the air. It ran to safety, dragging its damaged leg. While many monsters had been killed, one thing was certain in the whirling, seething mass. Jarrow's snarling brutes vastly outnumbered the wolves and Forest creatures. Verian clasped her wooden rod tightly, never taking her eyes off the fight.

Despair clawed at Gwen's throat. Verian would lose her wolves. Isa would die. The villagers would be killed or enslaved.

'What's that?' a tremulous voice called.

'More monsters?'

Gwen pivoted to the shouts. The villagers raised their arms, pointing into the leaden sky where the last wisps of fog were tinged with dawn's pale pink streaks. From the west, a beast with wide wings flew towards them. Wide, dark wings, huge tawny body, and a long tail. Two people rode the beast, clinging to its feathered neck.

Hope stirred in her chest. Asfal?

The Danae milled about, their fear of the flying creature adding to their terror of Jarrow's white monsters. 'What is it?'

'Will it kill us?' 'Another monster?'

Not Asfal, but definitely a gryphon. Gwen's heart leaped. One of the riders was a copper-haired boy.

'Connor!' she yelled.

***

'There's a fight going on.' Beron tugged at Connor's cloak – a gift from Lord Gryphon to replace the shabby fur – and leaned out over Nessus' side to peer into the Forest emerging from dawn's shadows. 'Monsters.'

Connor's gut twisted. 'That's the track between the villages,' he said. With growing horror, he recognised a familiar figure concentrating on the battle. 'There's Jarrow, controlling them.'

No Danae fought. Unless you counted the dark-haired lady standing near the battle with a wolf curled at her feet. Verian. Connor knew her, and her wolves, from the same pack which saved his Uncle Mark from tumbling to his death over a waterfall. During the times Connor had visited the Cavern-dwelling Danae with Aunt Gwen, his admiration for these beautiful creatures had grown. As had his respect. No cuddly, friendly, dog-like creatures these.

Verian watched the struggle as intently as Jarrow, paying no attention to the gryphon's approach.

'Are those boar fighting?' Beron said.

Yes. Nessus slowed his descent. *They're trying to destroy the loathsome creatures. Eagles have joined the battle too.*

Connor was heartsore at the sight of the outnumbered wolves and boar fighting to keep the monsters from the village. The snow on the track had been churned to mud, dark with blood.

'There are people, near the trees. They've seen us.' Beron gave the cloak another tug. 'They're scared.'

Connor shifted his gaze from the fighting to the villagers. They backed into the trees, waving pitchforks, shovels, pokers, shouting at Nessus.

'They think we're another monster.' It horrified him to cause this new terror. 'No one's seen a gryphon.' *Don't be* frightened, he wanted to call. It would be a waste of breath. Nobody would hear him above the noise.

One woman stood her ground, staring up. Aunt Gwen. Had she recognised him? A nervous giggle caught in his throat, dying at the sight of Matthew holding a person wrapped in a cloak close to his chest. They must be injured, or dead. Who was it? Again that despair.

Why aren't they destroying the attackers? Nessus asked, with a hint of irritation. *They don't need me.*

Connor gave a short, desperate laugh. 'Of course they need you. They're not Hunters. They don't have weapons, they can't fight. The monsters would kill them.'

No weapons? They carry iron. Don't they know about iron? It sounded like an accusation of stupidity.

'Know what?' Connor's mind spun. What did iron have to do with anything?

In the old legends, iron could vanquish creatures birthed by this evil. Nessus resumed his headlong flight to the ground. *Hang on!*

They landed in the snow between the cowering villagers and the fighting. Connor fell off Nessus, dragging Beron with him. The gryphon immediately lifted into the air and flew, not into the battle, but above the trees. Here he began a weaving, stately dance above the treetops, swooping into the branches and up again, as if he was trying to talk to the trees.

Connor had little time to watch and wonder.

Aunt Gwen reached him first, distracting him from Nessus' odd flight. She laughed, crying as she hugged him. 'You're safe, and look at you …' She held him at arm's length, her face wet with tears. 'Flying a gryphon, though where you found him …'

Connor's father snatched him from Gwen, hauling him into his strong arms, squeezing the breath from his body.

Connor struggled free. 'The iron.' He gestured at the home-made weapons. 'The creatures, it kills them. Nessus – the gryphon – told me.'

His father stared at him. 'What are you talking about? Gwen, have you heard about–?'

Aunt Gwen was already among the villagers. She moved from one to the other, touching their rough weapons. 'Iron will kill them. Go and fight. Your farm tools will kill them.'

The villagers hesitated. Connor squirmed, not blaming them. What if the weapons needed special iron? Imbued with Gryphon magic, say, or the spells of Sleih Seers?

Nessus had finished his aerial dance and joined the battle. He flew low above the creatures, beak, claws and talons ripping at white monsters, which evaporated at his touch. The exhausted wolves and boar drew back, but each time they stalled, a snarling beast jumped at them, cruel claws extended. They fought for their lives, defending themselves, weariness etched in every limb.

Connor's lungs filled with air. He whooshed it out and snatched a hay fork from the willing hands of an old man. Stumbling in snow growing wetter as the sun rose higher, he ran to the fighting. From the corner of his eye, he saw his father pick up a long mallet with a heavy iron head, one he used in the mill. He ran after Connor.

The villagers remained hesitant. Only Beron followed, flailing through the ankle deep slush, using a garden spade to keep himself upright. Connor stifled the image of what those monstrous claws would do to his friend. Praying Nessus was right, he charged into the melee, squeezed his eyes tight shut and laid about him with the hay fork.

No resistance slowed his weapon. He squinted his eyes partly open. His mad swipes must have missed, and why wasn't he lying in the mud with his stomach ripped out? A circle of emptiness surrounded him, the length of his weapon. He swung about. His father, too, and Beron, were upright, wielding the mallet and spade. Creatures lunged at them, falling on to the makeshift weapons. And dying instantly.

Beron whooped. 'It works!' He danced about, smashing the shovel into any bit of dirty white fur or skin he could find.

Connor's father, grim-faced, did the same.

Made brave by the sight of success, the villagers finally slipped and slid up the track. They came like a storm, whirling their farm tools, their spades and forks, their kitchen utensils, through the still, cold air. The white monsters fell to the iron's touch, one by one. The wolves and boar retreated, giving space to the battle-maddened Danae. Nessus dipped and clawed at the baying creatures, which melted into smoking piles of bones at the gryphon's magic touch.

'No!!' Jarrow's anguished cry rang above the clamour. 'You'll pay for this.' Red-faced, spitting vengeance, the captain strode unflinching through his dying army to advance on Connor. His upraised knife glinted. 'A witch like her,' he shrieked. 'All witches, damnation to you all.'

Connor flinched from the knife. The hay fork slipped from his hand. Jarrow reared above him, knife poised.

A hideous monster leaped for Connor. He ducked, from the knife, from the monster. The brute lunged, red mouth wide. It missed Connor and slammed into Jarrow. Its enormous claws ripped his bearded neck.

The captain's eyes widened. He slapped his hand to the welling wound.

Connor crouched on the ground, lungs bursting. He was aware of Beron beside him, keeping the remaining monsters at bay with his shovel. Connor's gaze stayed fixed on Jarrow.

The captain sank to the ground, eyes lifeless, a trickle of blood seeping between his chapped lips.

An enemy? Nessus hovered over Connor and Beron, his great wings sending draughts with each lift. He nudged Jarrow's body with his beak. *Even in his dead heart, I read a sorry tale of suspicion, arrogance, selfishness, and cruelty. The world is better off without him.*

'Are you hurt, son? Are you all right?' Peter knelt in the cold, wet mud, holding Connor's shoulders.

'I'm fine.' Connor gazed around, sobered to see victory with all its terrible cruelty.

'The forest, see the forest?' The cry came from one of the villagers. The fighters, panting, dripping with perspiration, rested on their home-made weapons. Their triumph glowed as brightly as the sun glinting off the snow lying heavy on the higher branches.

Now the Danae straightened, mouths open at the sight of huge trees wading from the Forest into the track.

'Oh,' Gwen said. 'Gryphon magic. It's happening again.'

Connor watched, his heart thudding with excitement, as vast oaks, beech, larch and alder swept over the battle-torn ground, bending their boughs to the fallen creatures. Nessus had woken them with his weaving dance.

The villagers stared, whispered.

'Just like before, when the Forest was reborn.' 'I remember.' 'Magic, they said.' 'Gryphon magic.'

The trees passed steadily, their great trunks moving easily through the churned snow. After they returned to the Forest all trace of the monsters had been erased. Jarrow's body, too, was gone. Verian's wolves remained, and the injured Forest wild creatures.

Each wounded animal struggled to right itself, and succeeded. Connor grinned. The wild creatures shook themselves and ran into the Forest. The wolves loped to Verian, forming a tight circle around her. She squatted to pat them, fondle their ears and generally treat them like puppies.

The villagers cheered.

One sight blotted Connor's joy. Matthew and his sad burden, and Aunt Gwen, were black figures trudging hurriedly to the village.

A bird sang. Another joined it. A chorus rose as if it was mid-summer dawn. Connor's heart swelled and tears wet his cheeks. He was home.

'We did it.' Beron jiggled, grinning. 'We did it, Connor. And I was brave, wasn't I?'

'You were.' Connor lurched to his feet to hug the boy, smiling. 'But were you scared?'

'Petrified. Scared stiff.'

Chapter Twenty Nine

The battle for the gryphon pendant

At the base of the Citadel, guards wielded swords and battle axes to hack at hideous white cat-like creatures with yellow eyes and red mouths. When the creatures fell at the touch of iron, more came, pressing the defenders hard against the great oak gates.

Archers stood at the parapet, taking careful aim, releasing their iron-tipped arrows with deadly effect.

Reptilian creatures clung to the walls, their forked tongues flicking ahead in search of prey. Green fire flashed down to destroy them.

Callie, with other Seers, moved swiftly between the weary casters of the green fire, giving what strength they could. All morning, the gryphon pendant had lain warm at her throat, imbued with new Sleih spells. As the battle raged on, and on, the jewel cooled with each giving. King Ieldon had ordered Callie to stay within the walls. Whatever power remained in the pendant, he – and Callie – did not wish the tiny jewel to fall into Melda's hands, however diminished its magic appeared to be.

Callie stopped briefly to gaze out across the battlefield. The white horde writhed and buckled like a dirty white blanket, scarcely a gap between the creatures. Silhouetted as dark shadows against a louring grey sky which threatened snow, Elrane, Mark, and their soldiers flew low over the monsters, cutting and slashing. As many of the monsters they slew, countless remained.

Further away, a handful of guards led Sleih and Madach

volunteers who had marched from the tunnel in the night and fanned out behind the white army to attack from the rear. The scarcely-trained volunteers were armed with maces, axes, pikes and war hammers – weapons hastily crafted from the iron Thrak and his new miners had hewn from the tunnel, cast in new forges by apprentice blacksmiths hurriedly learning their trade. Callie prayed the iron would protect the wielders.

In the midst of the melee, Ieldon on his flying horse skimmed the monsters, his purple cloak streaming behind him, his sword waving. He strove to reach Melda.

The Seer stood on a low rise, surrounded by her favoured monster bears, her bronze rod upright. The diamond at the rod's tip threw out a bright white light which cast a halo around its owner. Ieldon, and the small force of soldiers with him, slowly, slowly slashed a path to the rise. The gap seemed to Callie both too far and too close, for she feared Ieldon's magic could not withstand the combined force of the Seer and the Evil which worked its dreadful desires upon her.

Callie, we need you. Your promise to us, remember?

The voice of the fox – the one which had rescued the sheep from the monsters the day the refugees fled into the Citadel – sounded clear in Callie's head. Distress and fear marked it.

I hear, she called, searching the battle for the source. There. The leafless hedge which had sheltered the fox and his vixen was alight with fire, bright red sparks glinting in the winter gloom. The only escape must take them into the middle of the fighting, which would likely be death.

We have young, newly born. Can you help?

Carrying cubs, death was certain. Callie looked about her – at the exhausted Seers, at the sweat-drenched archers, and across the fighting to where Ieldon battled to reach their enemy. It was close by the burning hedge.

She thought, achingly, about her own family. Were they truly Jarrow's captives, or dead? Here, amid the fighting, was a family Callie could help. Besides, a promise was a promise.

Callie ran along the walkway, down the steps and along the Citadel wall to a corner turret. Here, a small door led outside. Throwing all her weight, and a little magic, at the heavy wooden bars holding the door closed top, bottom and middle, Callie shoved hard. The bars lifted, the door juddered, scraped, stuck fast, creating a gap barely wide enough for her to squeeze outside.

She touched the pendant, whispered, 'They can't see me, they can't see me,' praying the old chant – her first magic – held good.

Thick ropes of ivy covered the door. Callie pushed them aside, closing her mouth and eyes against the wet, cold leaves. She was through, at the top of a short, steep, ice-rutted slope, deep in shadows and mercifully free of fighting. To her left, Melda's diamond glowed in the snow-laden gloom. Ieldon fought to reach the Seer, his sword cutting down endless monsters. Fewer soldiers fought with him. He couldn't hold much longer.

Hurry, Callie. The fox's desperation caught at her mind.

I'm coming. Keep talking so I can find you.

Muttering her 'can't see me' chant, Callie slid down the ice, righted herself and ran into the battle. Her hands grasped her cloak tightly around her as she wove between terrible, deformed creatures, and dodged soldiers and their flashing swords.

Panting heavily, she reached the burning hedge. The fox and his vixen, a cub each in their mouths, crawled along the bare earth between the roots. Flames flared behind them.

I'm here. Callie lifted the tiny cubs from their parents to fold them in her cloak.

'Can't see me, can't see me,' she muttered, her heart beating rapidly in time to the words.

Hide in here, she said to the fox, opening her cloak to wrap about the two of them. *I'm taking you to where I came out of the wall. There's thick ivy at the top. You'll be safe there.*

The warm fur of the foxes brushed her legs as Callie, trying not to trip over the two, hurried back. They reached the slope, she bent to return the cubs to their parents, and straightened, readying to climb the slippery ice–

Well, well, well. A rescue mission. The witch and her wild creatures. How sweet.

Callie spun about as Melda's mocking tones lanced her head ...

... in time to see a huge, muddy, blood-streaked bear drag King Ieldon from his horse. Callie gasped in horror.

***

'Who's winning?' Willow, flying on golden-winged Theia, peered at the battle.

'No one,' Rowan shouted from his seat on a violet-winged young gryphon. 'They must have worked out about the iron, though. Like Lord Gryphon told us. See?' He pointed to a cluster of men in plain clothes standing back-to-back, brandishing pikes and maces at attacking monsters. 'Those aren't soldiers, they're ordinary people.'

Shall we help? Theia the Hunter didn't wait for an answer. She dived into the horrific creatures, talons and claws extended.

Willow held on, her hair and cloak streaming into the darkening sky. Theia raked the monsters. They didn't simply die at her touch. They vanished in a puff of black smoke, vanquished by Gryphon magic.

Willow would have cheered, but the cheer stuck in her throat at the sight of the undulating wave of dirty white pelts and skins which filled her view. Even on the walls of the Citadel, swarms of great white lizard-looking creatures crept upwards. Green fire rained down on them, yet still they came.

More gryphons joined the battle and more monsters evaporated into nothing. The sea of monsters seemed endless, yet the gaps between them widened under the fierce attack. Rowan waved Celeste, leaning from his violet-winged mount to add the sword's magic to the destruction. Willow let her cheer come. They would win this.

As the gryphons dived, they sent slim tongues of green and silver fire curling from their wings into the pikes and maces. The fighting men faltered, staring at the flying beasts and their flames. Until they saw the destruction these new fighters wrought. They whooped, triumph strengthening their cries. They fell to with greater energy with magic-imbued weapons which melted the enemy to nothing.

As more and more monsters disappeared, sooty flakes rose into the air, carrying a scent like cold, oily ash.

Ahead of Willow, Lord Gryphon flew straight, not engaging in the battle. Willow peered ahead, squinting in the gloom. A white light glowed on a low rise, casting a bright aura around Lady Melda.

Grandfather had fought his way close to the lady. He was nearly upon her.

'No!' Willow screamed.

A massive bear with a jagged lump on its head reached high with its brutish paws. It lunged, pushing Grandfather from his horse.

'Grandfather!' Willow's shout carried above the noise of the yowling, baying monsters. She buried her head against Theia, sobbing.

***

Callie ran, slipping in churned up slush, around fallen soldiers and monsters, towards the king. As she ran, a stranger's deep voice came to her.

Have courage, Callie, we are here.

She stared up. Her sharp grief at the king's fall blended with awe at the sight of gryphons filling the dusk sky. They dived among the monsters, and where they touched, clouds of black smoke rose. A scent, like cold ashes, stinking of death and evil, hung in the air.

Before she reached the king, a huge, black-winged gryphon swooped to where he had fallen. Clouds of acrid ash burst into the air. The gryphon rose from the ashes, Ieldon slumped over its lion back.

Callie's heart beat wildly.

Melda stood on her rise, arms straight at her sides, shouting at her beauties to finish their work and be done with the useless king.

Her beauties leaped at the gryphon. It flew high, out of reach of their cruel talons, and raced towards the Citadel. The soldiers who had fought to help the king clear a way to the Seer wheeled their horses to join the battle elsewhere.

Melda screeched her displeasure at the king's rescue. She twisted to where Callie stood, exposed, unable to move.

We meet again, little witch. Her voice quivered with rage. Her green eyes flashed their hatred. *And this time I will have the pendant.*

She strode from her hill, the bears flowing around her.

Callie clutched the silver gryphon. She should run, fast. She should call on the power of the Seers casting their magic death from the walls. Her leaden legs refused to move. Her head filled with mist, thoughts falling into chaos. She waited for death from those claws.

Hold, Callie. Resist her.

The strange, deep voice pierced the fog. The pendant grew warm in Callie's grasp. She lifted her hand from it, watching, helpless, as Melda approached, surrounded by her swarming monsters.

The black-winged gryphon had returned. It hovered above Melda, flanked by more of its kind. Their wings beat steadily in the darkening sky. They opened their great beaks, sending out a noise like a thousand bees. The soft, steady drone carried magic, flowing in brightly coloured ribbons, wafting to Callie, seeking the pendant. The silver pendant swelled and shone, its light matching the diamond on the tip of Melda's bronze rod. The heat of the jewel against Callie's neck nourished her own magic, shredding the mist filling her mind.

Melda strode forward. 'They do my job for me.' Her red-lipped grin split her face. 'Magic to swell my own, for the Great Spirit to feast on.'

Callie stared into Melda's deep green eyes. A coldness tightened in her skull, squeezing, hurting ...

You must hold, Callie, you must hold!

'It's mine!' Melda shrieked. 'I will have it at last, not you, you unworthy Danae witch.' Her hand reached for the jewel, her eyes triumphant.

With a great effort, Callie jerked back, her hand grasping the pendant. Heat spread from her fingers, along her arms, filling her body. And filling her mind too, warming and easing the cold tightness there.

Melda's icy hands grabbed Callie's fist, tugging. 'Release it,' she hissed. 'Its power is wasted on your pathetic so-called magic.'

The Seer's touch sent new, excruciating pain searing Callie's mind. She wanted the pain to stop. If she gave Melda the jewel the pain would go away. It hurt so much. She wanted the pain to go away …

A soft breeze wafted against her hair. A hot breath reached her cheek.

Hold, dear heart.

Asfal! Asfal was here.

Callie's heart soared. She strove to bend the pain of Melda's piercing gaze, focusing it on the jewel filled with fresh, strong Gryphon magic, letting the magic carry the pain away.

'I will have it!' Melda screamed.

'Never,' Callie whispered. She tore her gaze from Melda's glare and fell against Asfal who stood behind her, claws and paws firmly planted. She let go of the pendant, allowing it to shine freely.

Melda grabbed for it. Her hands were stayed, held by an invisible vice. She growled, deep in her throat like one of her own monsters. Her hands shook. Streams of green and silver light streaked from the swollen silver gryphon. They swirled around the Seer. She stumbled, steadied herself. Raising the bronze rod she cried into the air.

'Great Spirit! I have set you free! Join with me!'

Heavy black smoke rose from the trampled snow, whirled about Melda. A ferocious grin lit her face.

Callie's breath stopped in her throat.

The green and silver magic mingled with the smoke, a whirlwind of dark and light. In the midst, Melda stood with arms outstretched, beckoning Callie.

'Come little witch. This is the end. See my strength?'

***

'Theia, what's happening?' Willow watched the spiralling dark and light smoke which eddied around the Seer. Was it good, bad?

Theia and the violet-winged gryphon carrying Rowan had held back from those gathered about Lord Gryphon. *No place for children,* Theia had muttered, swooping in for another kill of the monsters rapidly thinning below them.

They battle for power. Theia flew in a wide circle around the Seer and Callie. *Our magic against the ancient Evil which came out of Arneithe, woken again.*

'Who's winning?' From where Willow sat, the black smoke appeared to be devouring the green and silver. Her heart thumped.

Theia beat her wings harder, lifting Willow from the swirling magic. She didn't answer.

***

The drone from the gryphons grew louder, more intense. The green and silver ribbons from the pendant widened, shimmered brighter for an instant, then dulled.

Despair beat in Callie's chest. The Evil would win. Melda's magic would hold sway.

Asfal murmured into Callie's hair. *Once before we beat her. We are stronger now. Stay with me, dear heart. We will triumph.*

Dear heart. The buzzing drone soothed Callie's fogged mind. She reached deep inside herself, bringing out her love for Asfal, for her family, for the king, for Willow and Rowan. She poured her love into the shining silver gryphon which glowed, luminous, like a full moon in a starless winter sky.

The streams of Gryphon magic broadened, glimmered more brightly. They wound ever tighter around the black smoke, slowly, slowly extinguishing it, binding Melda with gleaming green and silver.

The Seer's grin vanished. Her eyes grew black with fury. Blue flames erupted from within the glowing bands tightening around her. 'Great Spirit. Join me!'

A black curl of dense smoke met Melda's furious plea. It spiralled from within the blue, green and silver.

Bright streams of Gryphon magic lit the growing darkness with green light. They devoured the smoke. The blue flames wavered.

Melda attempted to lift her bronze rod, calling on the Spirit to protect her. The rod's diamond tip blazed – a shaft of silver light which quickly died, quenched by the green ribbons of magic.

Horror scarred the Seer's unblemished skin. Her golden face paled and wrinkled like a crumpled parchment. The blue, the green, the darkness all exploded into the dusk.

Callie squeezed her eyes shut, clung to Asfal, buffeted by a fierce wind. When the wind passed, she opened her eyes. The maelstrom of magic had burned itself out.

Melda was gone.

As was her monstrous white army. A stink of cold ashes, greasy, acrid, smirched the air for a moment, and then that too was gone.

The snow which had threatened all day, fell at last, soft flakes drifting to the ground to cleanse the scarred earth. Callie filled her lungs with icy, fresh, delicious-tasting air. She wanted to laugh, to dance, to sing. She threw her arms as far as they would reach around Asfal's neck.

'I'm so very, very glad to see you, my friend. Alive.'

Asfal humphed. *Gryphons do not die easily.*

All across the battlefield, soldiers brought their exhausted horses to land, and guards stood leaning heavily on their weapons in the falling snow. The Citadel walls were free of white reptiles, pale green scorch marks staining the stone as a reminder of the struggle. On the battlements, Seers and archers wearily raised their arms in victory. Their cheers carried to Callie as she stood, tears wetting her face, beside Asfal.

Mark ran to them, grinning like a ten-year-old with a new toy, the shoulders of his cloak powdered with white flakes.

'Well done, little sister. Well done.'

Callie touched the silver pendant, shrunk to its normal size. The jewel had changed. Instead of lying on its side, beak closed, the tiny gryphon faced forward, wings wide. Its mouth had opened in a snarl, a tiny ruby tongue barely visible.

THE END

Epilogue

King Ieldon recovered from his attack by the monstrous bear, carrying a deep scar on his cheek for the rest of his long life. As he said to Callie, 'This scar will remind me Evil should not be tolerated. I should never have allowed Melda to retain any vestige of her power when Elrane and I stripped her of magic on the docks of Etting.'

'You couldn't foretell,' Callie said, 'she would seek an Evil we believed, if we considered it at all, was more legend than fact.'

Ieldon had given her his half-smile. 'If there's anything we've learned from our own recent history, it's that legends come true all the time.'

Connor achieved his dream of studying in the Citadel with his aunt. While he was sad to leave his parents, he was secretly relieved to be away from the Danae villages. The story of his arrival in the middle of a ferocious fight on a huge black-winged gryphon, and how his knowledge of what iron did to monsters had given victory to the Danae, forever silenced the bullies. He became a local hero, which he considered to be almost worse.

Beron, on the other hand, decided he had no desire to be a Seer after all. By the time Tristan arrived in a Madach ship to collect his son from the Danae, Beron was desperately homesick for the fields and orchards of Etting, its busy port, and its small castle. On the journey home across the southern oceans, Tristan told Beron the whole tale of Callie's Wild Army and his own role in ensuring Captain Jarrow didn't enslave the Danae. Beron was very proud to be Tristan's son.

When they returned to Etting, the first thing Beron did was hug Dash and remove the ribbons in the pony's mane and the paint from his hooves. Afterwards, he dragged his father to the roof of the castle's tower. From this high point, he wondered at the beauty of the small but perfect duchy, as Tristan's mother used to call it, and vowed to devote himself to his studies and be a good son and heir, which pleased his tutor.

Isa never returned to the robber Madach. Her shoulder healed thanks to Gwen's ministrations, but the wound often ached. Gwen offered to continue making poultices to ease the pain, so it made sense for Isa to stay with the Danae. Matthew was an attentive visitor, concerned for the woman he had carried to safety in the aftermath of the deadly fighting. When the two eventually realised they were in love, they married – the first Danae and Madach marriage in many, many years.

This time, the villagers didn't forget who saved them from Captain Jarrow. Elder James was politely asked to step aside as Senior Elder, or as an Elder at all. He spent his time in his large cottage, where it was said he was writing a memoir 'to tell the truth about everything'. Whether it was ever finished, no one cared.

Matthew was persuaded to take James' place. He served the Danae well with his Council which included Peter, Lucy, and Gwen (and Isa unofficially).

Thrak's joy was boundless at discovering gryphons existed in the world after all. He asked Lord Gryphon to allow him to visit the 'new' caverns (as he called them). Lord Gryphon said yes, and when Thrak showed no sign of leaving, he never mentioned it. Thrak was content to mine new tunnels, hewing gems from the depths for the gryphons to use in their magic, as they had ever done. The gryphons considered he more than earned his keep among them.

Asfal visited his fellow gryphons more often than he used to. Willow and Rowan would frequently go with him, and occasionally Lord Gryphon would make a return visit to the Citadel to talk with his old friend, Ieldon. As the years went by, it was Willow who spent most time in the caverns high in the alps. Steeped in Gryphon magic, she became a wise and powerful Seer, and Rowan's chief advisor when the day finally came for him to take up the Sleih throne.

The foxes made themselves a den within the ivy under the walls where they raised several litters. On fine summer evenings, Callie would often squeeze through the forgotten door in the turret and push her way between the ropes of ivy. She would sit on the slope playing with the cubs and chatting to the foxes. Or she would gaze out to where a burning hedge had led to the greatest test of her faith in her magic.

After one of these ponderings, Callie understood she had an important task to undertake. During the following winter she added new chapters to the great book, *The Ancient History of the Old Sleih and How They Came by Their Magic through Ponderous Schemes and Long Collusions with the Fabled Gryphon of the High Alps of Asfarlon.* These chapters told the tale of the Winter of the White Horde. She wrote them in the common tongue of the Sleih and Madach to make sure the lessons they contained were unambiguous – just in case future generations had need of them.

Glossary

While *Winter of the White Horde* can be read as a standalone, this glossary will act as a reminder to those who have read the previous four books, and give further help to those who haven't. I haven't been exhaustive with characters, outlining only those important to *Winter of the White Horde*.

The Danae: As told in *Quests*, Book Two of Guardians of the Forest, the Danae are a race formed from the intermarriage of Madach and Sleih, after the time of *Legend of the Winged Lion*. For reasons explained in the books, they are expelled from the Kingdom of the Sleih and sent east into the Deep Forest of Arneith to find a new home. They live as a small, isolated community on the edge of the Forest, where the great southern oceans meet the coast. At the time of Guardians of the Forest they have faded from history for the Sleih and Madach, who believe them a myth.

The Gryphon: in *Legend of the Winged Lion*, the gryphons are known for their love of poetry and the arts, and all things beautiful; and for the magic they work with gems mined from the tunnels below the caverns of Asfarlon. During the battle against the Evil, the gryphons lose their power of speech. They do not follow the Sleih to the High Plains, but instead found themselves a new home in another group of caverns further east and south in the Alps.

The Sleih: a long-lived race with various magical skills. The more they practise their magic, the longer they live. They are distinct physically, with golden skin, deep green eyes and black hair. In the prequel, *Legend of the Winged Lion*, the Sleih live with the Gryphon in beautiful, comfortable caverns in the High Alps of Asfarlon. But, as told in that story, their home is destroyed in the battle against an old Evil which is accidentally summoned. Afterwards, the Sleih move down onto the High Plains and build the Citadel of Ilatias, as the centre of the Kingdom of the Sleih.

The Madach: the people who comprise the main population of this world. They have no magic, and are primarily farmers, artisans or work in the professions, such as the law.

Main Characters

Guardians of the Forest trilogy

Callie: a young Danae girl who discovers the magic within herself when her forest home is invaded by the Madach. She also befriends a baby gryphon, later called Asfal, who is the offspring of the dying gryphon which guarded the Forest.

Gwen, Lucy, Mark: sisters and brother of Callie, who have their own adventures as part of the Guardians trilogy.

Tristan: son of the Madach **Lord Rafe of Etting**, an empire-builder who sends men to fell what he believes is the uninhabited forest for fuel for his weapons' manufactories. He orders Tristan, who loves trees, to accompany the party to toughen him up. Tristan defies his father by helping Callie and the wild creatures save the Forest and the Danae escape being taken into slavery by the Madach invaders.

Captain Jarrow: the Madach leader of Rafe's invaders. When he discovers the 'fairytale' Danae he immediately plans to enslave them and sell them off to Madach lords and ladies.

Elder James: a Danae senior elder who secretly allies himself with Captain Jarrow in the plan to enslave his own people, in return for unstated rewards.

Lady Melda: a Seer of the Sleih, and a member of the King's Council with grand ambitions for power. She allies herself with Lord Rafe as a means to an end. To augment her power, she is desperate to possess the ancient gryphon pendant which Gwen was given as a charm, not knowing its powers. When Melda is unmasked as a traitor, the king, Ieldon, and his son take away her magic. Jarrow, a prisoner of the Sleih himself, witnesses this event after he is freed.

King Ieldon: the king of the Sleih who, with Gwen, Mark and Lucy, takes a small group of soldiers to the rescue of the Danae and to stop the destruction of the Forest.

Isa: A Madach robber girl whom Gwen befriends when she and Mark are captured by Isa's people to be sold as fairytale slaves. Isa helps them escape and warns of a further, Melda-inspired attempt to capture them (and the pendant) when they are travelling with the king back to the Danae.

Verian: the niece of the dour Queen of the Caverns in the Deep Forest, and the mistress of a wolf pack. She becomes Gwen and Mark's friend when she helps them escape her aunt, who believes them to be spies.

Prequel, *Legend of the Winged Lion*

Olban: a Seer of the Sleih whose quest for more and more magic leads him to accidentally awaken, and then be taken over by, an ancient Evil asleep in the deepest depths of the caverns of Asfarlon where the Sleih and Gryphon live.

Ilesse: a young, highly gifted Sleih apprentice Seer. She is touched by the ancient Evil, and must battle its tempting promises to give her 'her heart's desires' if she allies herself with it.

Thrak: a Sleih miner. He guides Olban and a small party of Sleih Seers into the tunnels to purportedly seek the reasons for unusual disturbances there. Olban, now a creature of the Evil, leads Thrak and the party into the Evil, where the Seers are transformed and Thrak is assumed to have died.

Afterword

I began this sequel several years ago, not long after the initial publication of the Guardians of the Forest trilogy. Somehow, it was overtaken by the prequel, *Legend of the Winged Lion*, published in early 2022. After releasing *River Witch*, a book for grownups, in September 2022, I decided it was time to round out the Guardians' tales, and here we are.

It's been fun delving into the various stories and bringing bits of all four books into this one. Sometimes I wonder at the unconscious minds of writers, where we discover events or objects we write about in earlier books unexpectedly come in useful. Who knew at the time Ieldon gave Isa a ring in gratitude for her help, that this ring would prove such a useful plot device in a story set twenty years later? Not this author.

While it's unlikely there will be more Guardians' books, I suspect another fantasy – maybe for grownups – might come out at some point. They're fun to write, and the research mostly comprises being steeped in lore, legend and fairytales. My kind of research.

Cheryl
November 2023

What next?

If you have enjoyed this story please take a few minutes to leave a review or a rating on Amazon or Goodreads. Reviews are important to independent authors who don't have the might of publishing companies to help get their books known. You could also recommend it to a friend.

If you haven't already, do read the *Guardians of the Forest*. And the prequel, *Legend of the Winged Lion*. You'll be amazed at how much you'll recognise. All my books are available on Amazon kindle unlimited to read for free.

The Wild Army Book One

Callie's forest rings to the thwack of enemy axes. When she searches for help in the secret places of the forest, she discovers her own magic. Will it be enough?

'The twists and turns of the story keep you reading, wondering who to trust, what might happen next and what it all means for the Danae.' Amazon review

Quests Book Two

Gwen and Mark battle wolves, robbers and the dangers of the Deep Forest in their quest for the mythical Sleih. But all will be lost if a powerful Seer finds them first.

'I couldn't put it down and read the whole book in one sitting. I highly recommend this book and series.' Amazon review

Gryphon Magic Book Three

When Gwen, Mark and Lucy reach the Forest with the Sleih rescuers, they find ruin and desolation. Can the Forest be redeemed from the invaders' destruction?

'My granddaughter and I have read all three books because we just had to know how the story was going to end. We were not disappointed.' Amazon review

Legend of the Winged Lion - Prequel

Ilesse's destiny is to be a powerful Sleih seer. But when Evil touches her, she must battle its whispered promises – or see her world destroyed by her own hand.

'Cheryl Burman's magic touch brings evil to life in a battle not all will survive. This is what can happen when dreams come true.' Goodreads review

Acknowledgements

I am, as ever, grateful to Jodi and Paula, my wonderful critique partners and friends, for being with me chapter by chapter as I wrote this book. Your advice on everything from plot sticking points to commas is invaluable.

Also many thanks to Dean Writers Circle's novel group for their comments and suggestions, and for enjoying the tale as it unfolded.

And, finally, to my husband David, who patiently turns my scribbles into real books and my vaguely described – with hand gestures to clarify – ideas into covers which readers love.

About the author

Originally from Australia, Cheryl Burman now lives in the Forest of Dean, UK, and, like Tolkien, Rowling and many others, the Forest inspired her to write. She started with middle grade fantasy, discovered a taste for historical fiction, and has more recently moved on to historical fantasy, which she rather likes. Given she is lucky enough to live in a place chock-a-block full of history, legend and myth, there is much to draw on. Two of her novels have won awards, as have several of her flash fiction pieces. Some of these are included in her collection, *Dragon Gift*, while others are published in various anthologies. A keen student of writing craft, Cheryl has had articles published on writing-related topics both online and in print and maintains a popular writing tips post on her blog.

As Cheryl Mayo, she is the chair of Dean Writers Circle and a founder of Dean Scribblers, which encourages creative writing among young people in her community.

All her books, including purchase links, can be found on her web site.

Cheryl's monthly newsletter, *By the Letter*, keeps her readers up to date with her work, and offers short stories, bits of fascinating research, interviews with authors of interest, and local literary news.

Go to her web site to sign up and receive a free eBook as a thank you gift.

Website: cherylburman.com

Printed in Great Britain
by Amazon